Anakin Skywalker

Todd Strasser

SCHOLASTIC INC.

New York Toronto London Auckland Sydney
Mexico City New Delhi Hong Kong

ISBN 0-590-52093-8

Book designed by Madalina Stefan.

12 11 10 9 8 7 6 5 4 3 2 1 9/9 0 1 2 3 4/0

Printed in the U.S.A.

First Scholastic printing, June 1999

Anakin Skywalker

Introduction
Naboo

The battle is over. There is peace again on Naboo. Through my window I am watching the people of Theed clear away the rubble. Wrecked Trade Federation tanks and the burned battle droids are being towed off. Shattered statues are being put back together. The job of rebuilding this beautiful city will be hard, but the people of Naboo don't seem to mind. I think they are thankful that they are alive.

I am thankful to be alive, too. I could have been killed many times. I should be happy, but I'm not. A great man gave his life so that these people could live. I will never forget him.

That is why I am writing this journal. So much has happened . . . I'm afraid it's too much for me to fully remember. Yet I sense even greater and more important things are coming soon.

The air here on Naboo is damp and warm. As I sit beside the window, the sun feels good on my skin. It is so different from the place I come from.

I am only here for a while. I'm not sure what will happen when I leave, but until then, I will work on this journal.

My name is Anakin Skywalker.

I am nine years old.

First Entry
I Meet an Angel

Something strange happened to me. I was working in the junk heap behind the shop when Watto yelled at me to come inside. He is always yelling at me from under his long snout. He hovers around the shop on stubby blue wings that make a humming noise. He is my master and I am his slave. So I have to listen.

"Come into the store," Watto yelled. His store is just a dusty junk shop. Like most of the buildings here in Mos Espa, it is domed and made with thick walls to keep the heat out.

I usually work in the junkyard in the back. My job is to look for parts in the small mountain of busted-up space vehicles Watto has collected. Sometimes I hate the work, but it's taught me a lot. I doubt there are many nine-year-old Humans around Tatooine who know half as much about mechanical stuff as me.

I normally don't mind getting out from under Tatooine's two suns. Around midday they can really roast you. But just when Watto called me I was pulling a cooling unit out of a Podracer. I'd been looking for a cooling unit like it for weeks. I wanted to give it to my friend Jira, the old lady who owns the fruit stand in the marketplace.

I ran into the store. If there are customers, Watto always yells more. It's his way of showing off and proving to people what an important junk dealer he is. A small group of people and an astromech droid were inside. That was pretty unusual.

One of the people was an older man who looked like a farmer. He was tall and had a beard, long dark hair, and strange eyes. Right away I noticed he was different. He didn't have the scarred, calloused hands moisture farmers usually have.

There was also a creature who looked like a cross between many species. He stood upright on two legs like a Human. He had a mouth shaped like a bill, and a frog's big eyes rising out of his head. He was not really that unusual compared to some of the creatures who pass through Mos Espa. But I'd never met anyone like him before.

Tagging along with them was a small, blue, dome-topped R-2 astromech droid.

And finally, there was *her*. At first I didn't notice anything unusual because she was small and dressed in rough peasant clothes. But on second glance I noticed that, like the older man, something wasn't quite right about her. She was older than me, but not old. She may have been wearing coarse clothes, but there was something delicate about her. Her long, braided brown hair shimmered. There was a glint in her brown eyes and her skin was too perfect for a farm girl.

My heart started to beat a little harder, and I felt strangely drawn to her. It was unlike anything I'd ever felt before. I looked closer and instantly knew that she was the most beautiful creature I had ever seen. In fact, I was certain that I was in the presence of an angel, even though I'd never met one before.

Second Entry
Magnet for Trouble

Tatooine is probably the last place in the galaxy you'd expect to find an angel. It is a hot, dusty planet. And people don't follow the laws of the Galactic Republic here. Tatooine is run by the Hutts, who are known throughout the universe as gangsters and cold-blooded killers. Our planet is populated by misfits and criminals who have nowhere left to go. I think it is one of the few places in the galaxy where you can buy and sell slaves, like my mom and me.

A bunch of hyperspace trading routes meet here on Tatooine. This means we get visitors not only from our galaxy, but other galaxies as well. A lot of strange types come into Watto's junk shop looking for parts. We get bounty hunters, hired blasters, spice pirates, and all sorts of deep-space pilots traveling to and from places you've never heard of before and will probably never hear of again.

It was an old deep-space pilot who told me about the angels. He said they lived on the moons of Iego and were the most beautiful creatures in the universe. They were also supposed to be good and kind — two words you don't hear much on Tatooine.

Watto took the older man and the astromech droid out back to look for parts. That left me with the frog man and the angel. Of course, I didn't know *for sure* that she was an angel. I only suspected it. So I just sat on the counter and pretended to clean a transmitter cell.

The angel was sweating and she dabbed her forehead with a cloth. I had a feeling she wasn't used to the kind of heat we lived with on Tatooine.

She must have known I was staring at her because after a while she gave me a funny smile. That's when I asked her if she was an angel.

She looked surprised, then said she'd never heard of angels. I think she was telling the truth. So I told her maybe she was one and didn't know it.

We started to talk, and the next thing I knew, I was telling her that I was a pilot, and how Watto had won my mom and me from Gardulla the Hutt on a bet.

She seemed surprised to hear I was a slave.

Meanwhile, the frog man couldn't keep still. He poked through the bins and shelves. It seemed as if he had to touch everything in the shop! Finally he accidentally activated a small pit droid. The droid started marching, knocking things over, and dragging the frog man around the store.

It was a funny sight, and the angel girl and I laughed together. She had an easy laugh, and I knew I didn't want her to go away.

By the time Watto came back with the man and the astromech droid, I'd found out that the angel girl's name was Padmé. She knew my name was Anakin Skywalker. I was sad that the man was in a hurry to leave. I knew we had a lot of parts, so that must have meant that the man and Watto couldn't strike a deal.

Padmé and I said good-bye and she left with the others. Watto hovered around the shop complaining about how the outlanders always try to rip him off. His wings beat through the air so fast they were nothing more than a blue blur. But the good news was that all I had to do was clean some racks — then I could go home!

Of course, I didn't go home right away. Padmé may have left Watto's shop, but that didn't mean she was gone for good. As long as she was on Tatooine, I would find her.

* * *

The outlanders weren't hard to find, thanks to the frog man. You could tell he was a magnet for trouble. I found him in the market. He was lucky I did, because a Dug named Sebulba was about to squash him.

Sebulba was my archrival at Podracing. He's mean and ugly, with big eyes, long arms, and braids hanging down the sides of his head. Frankly, I don't care about looks. Once you've lived on Tatooine for a while, you've seen everything. But I do care about cheaters, and Sebulba was the worst.

Anything goes in Podracing. The only thing that matters is who crosses the finish line first. But some of us actually think it's wrong to mess with each other's Podracers. You should win by being the best and fastest pilot, not by knocking your opponent's Pod into a canyon wall on purpose.

But like I said, when it comes to cheaters, Sebulba is the worst in the galaxy. I wouldn't care that much except that in our last race I was winning . . . until he flashed me with his vent ports and practically got me killed.

Anyway, I found Sebulba standing over the frog man in the market. The frog man was squirming and trying to get away. But Sebulba wasn't about to let him. I hate to think about what would have happened if I'd gotten there a minute later.

I warned the Dug to back off. He wanted to

know why, and I told him that the frog man was connected to the Hutts. Dugs aren't the smartest creatures in the universe, but they know that messing with anyone connected to the Hutts can mean instant death.

Sebulba was mad, but he turned away from the frog man. He told me that the next time we raced he'd make sure I didn't live to see the finish line. I reminded *him* that if he killed me, he'd have to pay Watto for me.

Sebulba left, and I helped the frog man to his feet. That's when Padmé arrived with the older guy and the astromech droid unit.

They asked what had happened. I told them that Sebulba had picked a fight with the frog man and that I'd broken it up.

I guess the older man was surprised that I'd done that, because he gave me a strange look. As if he thought he saw something, but wasn't sure. It wouldn't be the last time he'd look at me that way. But it would be a while until I knew what it meant.

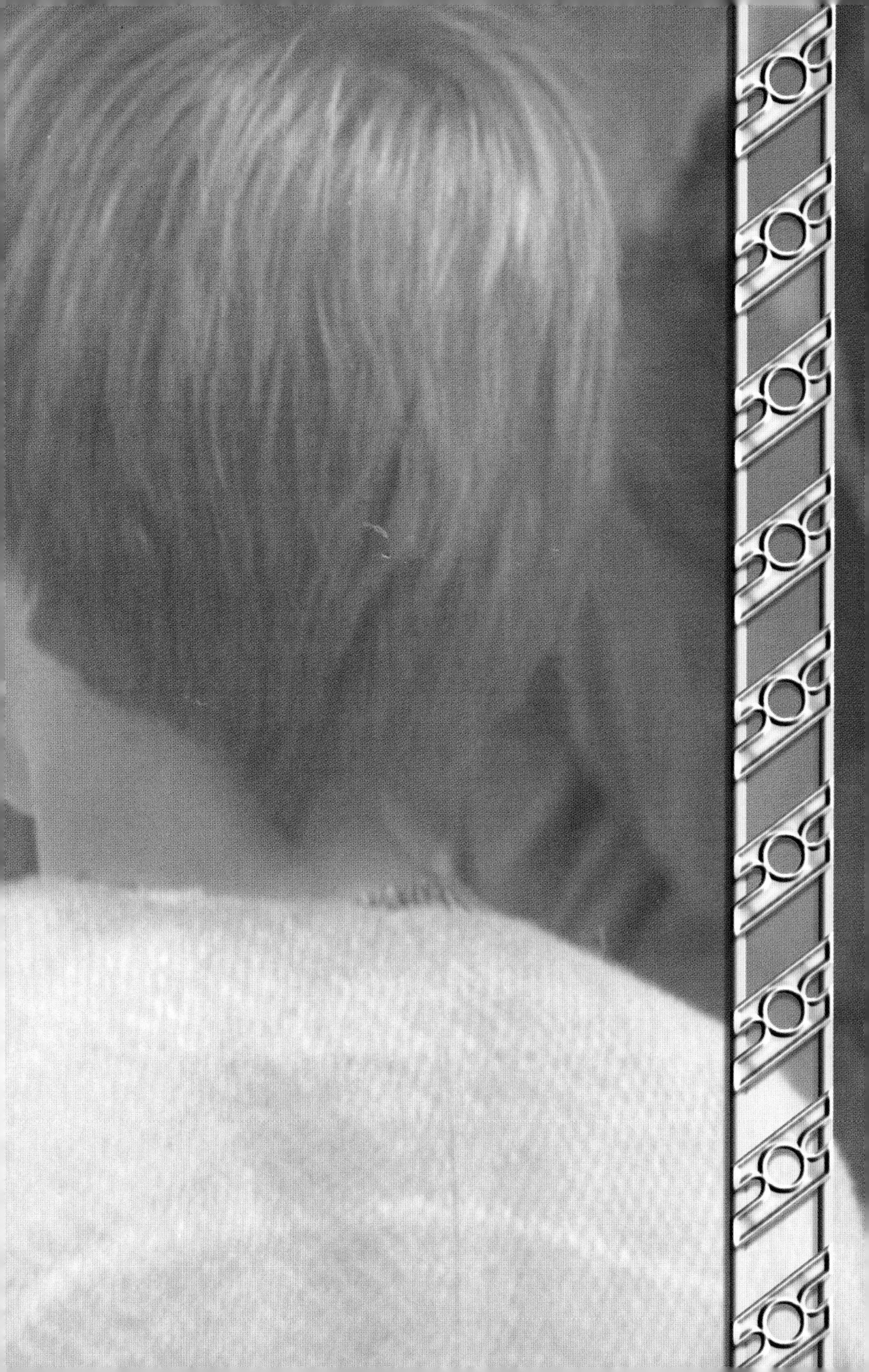

Third Entry
Jedi Secrets

We started to walk through the market. As usual, it was crowded with beings of every size and shape. Plus speeders, droids, and wagons pulled by eopies and giant, tame banthas. The man was still looking for the hyperdrive parts he needed for a J-type 327 Nubian. I was just glad to be with Padmé again. In a selfish way I hoped the man would have a lot of trouble finding the parts. Once he had that hyperdrive working, they'd all be going far, far away.

My friend Jira was up ahead. Her fruit stand was really just a ragged, sun-bleached awning stretched over a frame of poles. The awning provided shade for the fruit she sold. I thought since Padmé and the others were strangers here, they might like to try some local food.

Tatooine doesn't offer much, but we do have some interesting fruit.

Jira is old and bent, and has gray hair. Her clothes are patched and ragged, but they're always clean. The heat of the twin suns is hard on her. When I told her about the cooling unit I'd found in Watto's junk heap, she was really happy. Then I asked to buy four pallies. Pallies are sweet, juicy fruits grown at underground farms on Tatooine. I was pretty certain the strangers would like them.

As I took some truguts out of my pocket to pay for the fruit, one of the coins fell to the ground. The man bent down to pick it up, and I saw something amazing.

Under those farmer clothes was a *lightsaber!*

The kind only Jedi Knights carried.

I *knew* he wasn't a moisture farmer!

Now it was my turn to give *him* a funny look. But I made sure he didn't notice it. What would a Jedi Knight be doing here on Tatooine?

A gust of wind rippled the awning over Jira's fruit stand, and the old lady said she could feel a storm coming. Sandstorms happen a lot on Tatooine. They arrive fast and don't give much warning. They can be *very* dangerous. Already, sand and dust had begun to blow down the street, and some of the shop owners around us were starting to close their doors and take down their stands.

The Jedi Knight disguised as a farmer wanted to head back to his ship. But when I heard that they'd landed on the outskirts of Mos Espa, I knew they didn't have enough time to make it back safely. They'd be better off coming to my house and waiting until the storm passed.

I was glad when they accepted my offer. Not only would it give me more time with Padmé, I might find out what they were doing out here on Tatooine. After all, Mos Espa was a spaceport. It usually had plenty of available hangar space.

So why did they land in the desert?

Mom was surprised when she saw all the strangers in our hovel. But once I explained about the sandstorm she welcomed them to dinner. I introduced her to the others and learned that the Jedi Knight's name was Qui-Gon Jinn. The frog man's name was Jar Jar Binks, and the astromech droid was Artoo-Detoo.

Our home had one main room, plus two smaller rooms, where Mom and I each slept. What made it special was that my room was also a workshop. That's where I took Padmé as soon as everyone was introduced. I wanted to show her my latest project — a protocol droid to help Mom around the house.

My droid was named See-Threepio. He wasn't quite finished, but most of the circuitry and mechanics were done. He had arms, legs, and a head like a Human, but I didn't have the money or the parts for his outer shell. One day I hoped to cover him in gold chromium plating.

The funny thing was that the little blue dome droid Artoo-Detoo had followed us into my room. When he saw See-Threepio he started to beep and whistle.

See-Threepio blinked and spoke, "I beg your pardon . . . what do you mean I'm naked?"

Artoo-Detoo beeped again. I started to laugh.

"Oh, my goodness!" See-Threepio gasped. "How embarrassing! Am I really naked?"

Padmé grinned. I quickly explained to my protocol droid that he was only "sort of" naked and that I'd fix that problem soon.

I wanted to show Padmé the Podracer I was building, but it was outside in the storm, covered by a tarp. We went back into the main room instead.

We started to eat and talk. Padmé asked why, if we were slaves, we didn't go to a planet where we could be free? I had to explain about the transmitters that were hidden in our bodies and how we could be blown up if we tried to escape.

Padmé looked shocked. I knew then that she'd never encountered anything like life on Tatooine before. And it made me wonder. Where in the galaxy had *she* come from?

No one seemed to know what to say next. I figured Padmé was feeling sorry for Mom and me. And I don't like *anyone* feeling sorry for me. So I started talking about Podracing and how I was the only Human on Tatooine who could do it.

I could tell that Mom thought I was bragging, but I was just stating a well-known fact.

Qui-Gon said they had Podracing on Malastare. He knew it was very fast and dangerous.

And then he said that if I raced Pods, I must have Jedi reflexes.

I felt a chill. *Jedi reflexes?* I knew I was fast. But here was a real, live Jedi Knight hinting that I might be one of his kind! All of a sudden I felt the urge to tell him that I knew his secret.

But I hesitated. After all, he was dressed like a farmer. What if he didn't want anyone to know?

Everyone has secrets. Sometimes, if you spend enough time with someone, you can figure them out. That's how I knew Qui-Gon wasn't a moisture farmer and Padmé wasn't a farm girl.

I also had a secret. But mine was private. It had to do with the dreams I had. My dreams were different from the dreams of other kids I knew. Take my friends Kitster and Seek, for instance. They both wanted to be pilots like me. But they dreamed of leaving Tatooine forever and never coming back.

I dreamed about leaving, too. But I *would* come back. As a Jedi Knight. I dreamed about leading a slave rebellion here on Tatooine. I dreamed of holding a lightsaber, and of driving every last Hutt, criminal, and bounty hunter off this planet.

But I had another secret as well. A dark secret. It was about the way my dreams always ended. It was a secret that frightened me, one I could never tell.

I took a deep breath, and let it out slowly. I wasn't sure if I should say this, but I had to know.

"Qui-Gon," I said, "you must know what you're talking about, because you *are* a Jedi."

My mother gasped. The others around the table went silent.

Qui-Gon was quiet for a moment. Then he raised an eyebrow and asked why I thought that.

I said it was because I'd seen his laser sword.

"Maybe I killed a Jedi and took his lightsaber," he said.

I shook my head and said that couldn't be true. Everyone knew that Jedi Knights couldn't be killed.

Qui-Gon sighed. He gave me a look that would come back to haunt me.

"I wish that were so," he said.

I know now that I should have paid more attention to his words. But I was eager to tell him about my dream of becoming a Jedi and freeing the slaves on Tatooine.

Surely he, a Jedi Knight, would understand. I asked him if maybe that was why he'd come to our planet.

Qui-Gon slowly shook his head. And then he said that in fact they hadn't meant to come here at all.

For a moment I felt disappointed . . . until Qui-Gon explained that they were on their way to Coruscant.

Of all the places in the galaxy I wanted to visit, Coruscant was at the top of my list. From what I'd heard from spice pirates and deep-space pilots, it sounded like the exact opposite of Tatooine. Tatooine was a forgotten wasteland on the Outer Rim. Coruscant was the center of the galaxy. Tatooine was a near-empty desert. Coruscant was covered by an unending multileveled city. It was the capital of the Galactic Republic, and the home of the Jedi.

Qui-Gon explained that they were on a secret mission. But their ship was damaged and they'd had to land on Tatooine while they searched for parts. They would stay only as long as it took to repair the ship.

The problem was they didn't have the money to get the parts. Qui-Gon had plenty of Republic credits. But those were useless to Watto.

All of a sudden I had a great idea. The Boonta Eve Classic Podrace was in two days, and I knew I could win it. If Qui-Gon would enter me in the race, the prize money would pay for the parts they needed — and more!

Mom got upset because she hated when I raced Pods. And Padmé and Qui-Gon both agreed that they would try to find another way to get the money — one that didn't involve me having to risk my life.

But I wouldn't give up that easily. I reminded Mom of what she'd said so many times: that of all the problems in the universe, the biggest one was that people didn't help each other.

Mom started to shake her head, but then stopped. Our eyes locked. Without words, just using thoughts, I tried to tell her how important this was to me. That somehow, deep inside, I *knew* I had to race.

And then the most amazing thing happened. Mom turned to Padmé and Qui-Gon and said I was right. There was no other way to get the kind of money they needed. The only way was to let me race. She said she didn't like it, but that this was what I was meant to do.

Fourth Entry

We Prepare for the Race

There was still a lot to be done before I could race. First we had to scrape together the entry fee to get into the Boonta Classic. We waited until the next morning and then returned to the junk shop where Qui-Gon tried to make a deal with Watto.

That's when I knew how serious Qui-Gon's problems really were. To get the entry fee, he offered his ship.

Even Watto was smart enough to see what a great bargain Qui-Gon was offering him. If I won the race, Watto would get to keep everything except the parts Qui-Gon needed. If I *lost* the race, Watto got himself a Nubian starship.

Watto agreed, and we hurried back to my house to get my Pod ready for the race. Padmé,

Jar Jar, and Artoo-Detoo all pitched in. As we worked, I noticed Qui-Gon speaking quietly with my mom. I couldn't hear what they were saying, but from the looks on their faces and the way they kept glancing at me, I could tell it was serious.

Then the Jedi shook his head and Mom turned away with a sad look on her face. What was going on?

We kept working on the Podracer. It was *so* wizard! Two huge Radon-Ulzer turbines connected to a small trailing Pod by steelton control cables. You sit in the racer behind these monster engines and try to steer at speeds that can tear the hair right off your head. But for all its power and speed, the Podracer is an amazingly delicate machine. One nasty scrape against a rock formation or another racer, and you could disappear in a flaming bath of rocket fuel.

Some of my friends came over, including my best friend, Kitster. When I told them I was going to enter my Podracer in the Boonta Classic, everyone except Kitster laughed. They knew I'd been working on it for a long time. They also knew I'd never even gotten the engines running.

The others went off to play ball, but Kitster stayed behind, curious to see if I could actually get the Podracer to work.

In my heart I knew today was the day. I could

feel it. And when Qui-Gon gave me the power charge I needed, I got into the Podracer and inserted it.

I held my breath . . . and hit the ignition switch.

VARROOOOMMMM! The turbines roared to life. Red and pink energy binders flashed between the engine casings, and orange flames burst from the afterburners.

Kitster smiled. Padmé and the others cheered. I sat in the Pod, feeling the vibrations from those powerful turbines.

Boy, did it feel good.

But the job wasn't finished, and we worked straight into the night. And when we living creatures were too tired to work anymore, the astromech droid Artoo-Detoo kept right on going, throwing on a final coat of paint. By then it was way past my bedtime and Mom was hinting that I'd better get some sleep.

I agreed to stop for the night. But before I went to bed, I sat on the porch. I looked at all the stars in the night sky, and wondered which, if any, I would someday visit. Qui-Gon was dabbing some blood off a place where I'd cut myself. I was so busy imagining what it would be like to go out and visit all those systems that I almost didn't notice when he scraped some of my blood onto a comlink chip.

When I asked him what he was doing, he said he was simply checking for infections. I suspected there was another reason. But I knew that whatever it was, he wasn't going to tell me.

That night I had a new dream. I was someone powerful — like a Jedi Knight, but different. I was in a place I'd never seen before. A shadowy place. Padmé was there, but she seemed distant — older, and sadder. She was wearing battle dress, and while she still seemed delicate and perfect, she was also strong and determined.

She was leading a huge army into battle. And that was strange, too. I couldn't tell which side I was on.

When I woke in the morning, Padmé was there. I told her about the dream. She shook her head and said she hoped it wouldn't come true because she hated fighting.

Even though it was only a dream, I could tell that she took it seriously. As if somewhere inside her, she knew what I knew — that my dreams weren't just my imagination. That there was truth in them.

And sometimes that truth was frightening.

We went back to work on my Pod. Soon my friend Kitster showed up with two eopies. Those long-snouted pack animals would pull my Pod's turbines to the race arena out in the desert. I uncoupled the engines and hitched one behind each eopie. Artoo-Detoo would pull the Pod.

Kitster rode on one of the eopies while Padmé and I rode the other. I'd put on the jumpsuit Mom had sewn for me. As we slowly made our way through Mos Espa and toward the race arena, I tried to keep my mind on the race.

We got to the hangar where a dozen crews were preparing their racers. Good mechanics are hard to find out here. I never saw so many creatures pretending they knew what they were doing. One team had mounted their engines *backward!* Qui-Gon was already there, talking to Watto. Because of the clamor echoing through the hangar, I couldn't hear what they were talking about. But when Watto left he made a crack to me that I should warn Qui-Gon to stop betting before he ended up a slave, too.

Of course, when I asked Qui-Gon about it, he said he'd tell me later.

We got to work recoupling the engines to my racer. All around us the goofy crews of pit droids prepared their Podracers. Hydrospanners clanged against metal and delicate instruments fell to the floor with a crash. Nervous drivers screamed in frustration. The tension was understandable. The law of Podracing is unforgiving: Once the race begins, few will finish, and many will die trying.

It wasn't long before it was time to take the racers into the race arena. The arena is lined with viewing stands where the spectators gather to watch and bet. The turnout is always large because everyone loves to watch Podraces. Excitement is rare on Tatooine. On race days the crowded streets of Mos Espa are empty.

The race starts in the arena, then goes out into the desert canyons, then returns to the arena. Before it starts the racers bow to the "royal box." This was ridiculous. Jabba the Hutt, the biggest slime in the galaxy, sat in that box. And we had to bow as if he was some kind of king. The king of the crooks, maybe.

I knew if I lost the race, Qui-Gon, Padmé, and the others might be stuck on Tatooine for a long time. And when you were young and pretty on Tatooine, it wasn't long before you belonged to Jabba. To imagine Padmé chained like a slave made my blood boil.

I was distracted by the cheering when Sebulba's name was announced. He was considered the best Podracer on Tatooine, and everyone was betting on him to win the Boonta Classic again. And where was Sebulba? Hanging around near my racer. I gave him a warning look and he backed away, but not before he told me that I wouldn't live to see the end of the race.

It was time to begin.

If I said I wasn't nervous, I'd be lying. But I also knew I could do it. I'd raced against most of these creatures before. As long as my Podracer stayed in one piece and I kept away from Sebulba I could beat them all.

I put on my old helmet and goggles. Strapping my restraining belt down in the racer, I looked up at Qui-Gon's face. He asked if I was ready, and I told him I was. Then he told me to concentrate on each moment. He said not to think, but to trust my instincts.

Then he said, "May the Force be with you." And that's when I realized that as far as he was concerned, this wasn't just a race. It was also a test. Of me.

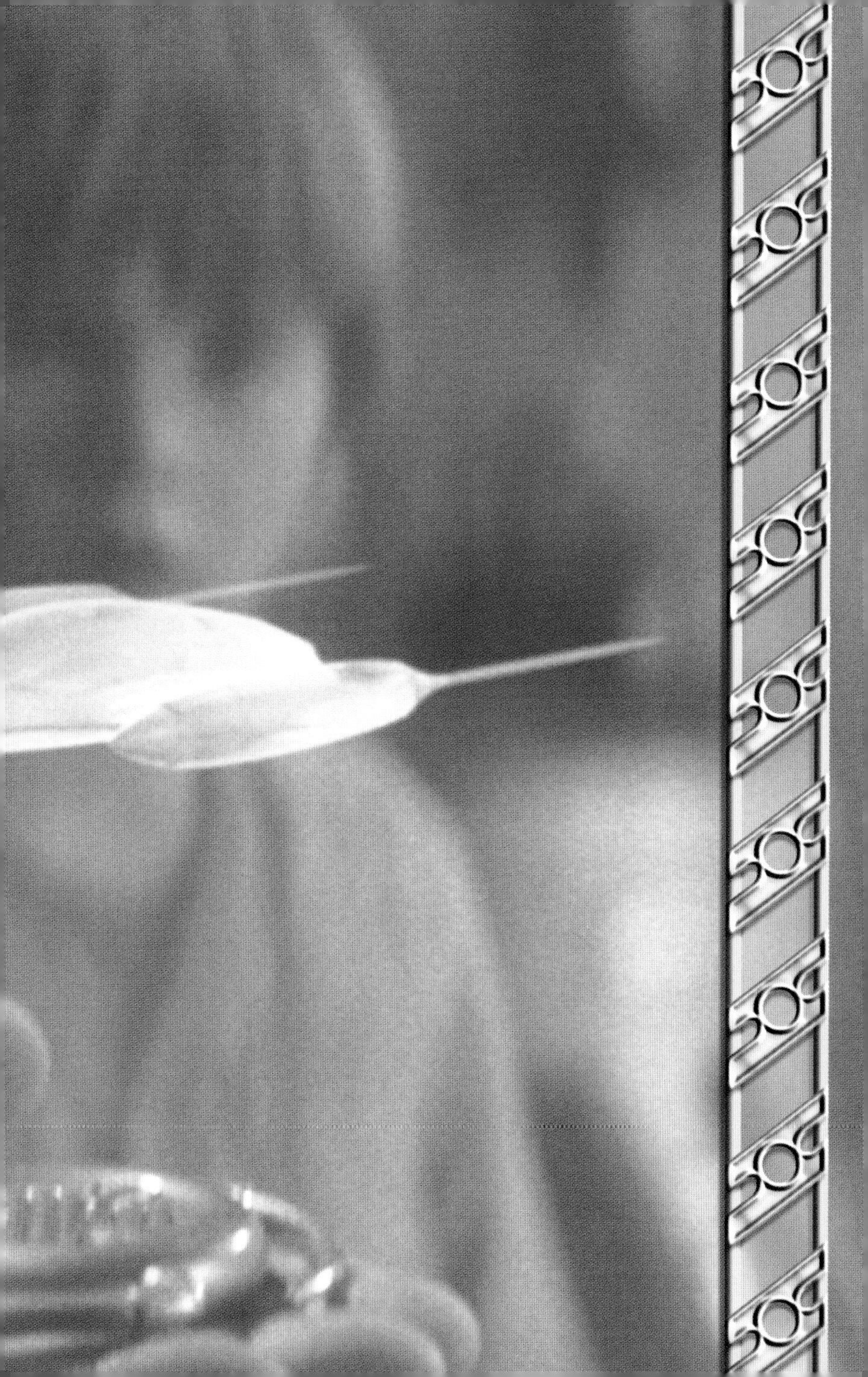

Fifth Entry
The Race of My Life

We started our engines. And let me tell you, there's no sound like it. The roar of a dozen Podracers is so loud it hurts your ears. It's like sticking your head inside a hyperdrive motivator. For me, that sound is pure adrenaline. It makes me want to go fast and win.

The starting light turned green and I pushed hard on my racer's thruster bars. The Podracers around me surged ahead in a pack. . . .

Meanwhile, with a sickening cough, my turbines went dead.

I sat there in the cloud of exhaust and dust as the other Podracers shot away from the starting line. I think that for a split second I was in shock.

Sebulba! All at once I knew he'd sabotaged my

engines. But it didn't matter. The only thing that mattered was getting back into the race.

I hit the starter again . . . and again. Tense seconds passed as I waited anxiously to see if the Radon-Ulzers would catch. Finally, with a sputter, they did.

I was off. Of course, I was way behind, but maybe that worked in my favor. Ahead I watched Sebulba's bright orange racer and Mawhonic's Pod go neck and neck into the first turn by the rock formations. Mawhonic didn't know what he was up against. If I'd had a comlink, I might have tried to warn him.

Too late. Sebulba veered into Mawhonic, sending him straight into the rocks. *Ka-boom!* Even at the back of the race I could hear the explosion as Mawhonic vanished in a huge ball of flame.

I know it must sound crazy, but all I wanted to do was catch up to the creature who'd just killed Mawhonic.

But first I had to pass the rest of the pack. Gasgano was the first challenge I faced. He was running a new ord pedrovia, which is really fast and agile. I tried to pass him, but he cut me off. Again and again I tried, but it wasn't until we dropped down off a mesa cliff that I put a move on him and slipped by.

Pang! Out of nowhere, something hit the back of my Podracer and made me swerve.

What the . . . ?

Then I saw them — four Tusken Raiders hiding in the canyon dune turn! They were cheering and dancing with delight. One of them must have gotten lucky with his projectile rifle and hit my racer. I gritted my teeth and shot past them.

Ka-boom! I heard another explosion and saw Sebulba racing away from a second huge ball of flame and smoke along the canyon wall. I didn't see what happened, but I knew that Xelbree had been trying to catch him a few moments before.

And now Xelbree was gone.

Ka-boom! Ody Mandrell cut too low over a dune and crashed. Now he was gone, too.

I felt a shiver. When you lost in this race, you lost everything . . . including your life.

The first lap was over. I told myself to be patient as I worked my way through the pack. Coming through the Arch Canyon for the second time, I was three hundred meters behind Teemto Pugales of Moonus Mandel when his racer suddenly exploded in a bright orange ball of fire.

Just like that, Teemto was gone, too.

By the beginning of the third lap I was in third place behind Sebulba and Terter. Obitoki and Habba Kee were right behind me. Terter was cagey enough to stay off Sebulba's tail, which was always a bad place to be. But as they came up through Jag Crag Gorge, Terter tried to sneak a

move that brought him too close. I knew what Sebulba was going to do even before he did it.

Thwank! Sebulba jettisoned a part. Terter couldn't avoid it. One of his engines sucked the part in and Terter veered *right into me!*

Whoa! The next thing I knew, my racer was out of control. Terter's vertical stabilizer had snagged the steelton line to my left engine, unhooking the main binding. Obitoki, Elan Mak, and Habba Kee slipped past while I whipped all over the sky, fighting to get my Podracer back under control.

To be honest, I thought I was a goner. Flying a Podracer with a loose engine is like hitching a ride on a comet. I figured if I didn't crash, I'd probably be pulled out into the upper atmosphere and freeze to death.

The other danger came from the loose steelton line. Flying free, it could snag a rock outcropping and swing me right into oblivion at any moment.

I kept fighting for control, working the stabilizer pedals with my feet — using the magnetic retriever to try and grab the loose line. But my Podracer was swinging wildly. It seemed hopeless until I remembered Qui-Gon's advice: *Feel. Don't think. Trust your instincts.*

By then I figured I had nothing to lose. . . .

I focused. *Stabilize. Catch the steelton line. Focus!*

I stopped thinking about it and just reacted.

And then I did something I'd never done before. As the Podracer swung toward the loose line, I reached out with the magnetic retriever and managed to grab it. An instant later I rehooked the line to the left Radon-Ulzer.

Suddenly I was back in control.

But this was the last lap and I'd lost valuable time. Would I still be able to catch up?

I passed Elan Mak.

Ka-boom! Ahead, Obitoki disappeared in flames and smoke. Sebulba had flashed him with his side vents, the same move he'd used on me in our last race, only I'd managed to crash-land and walk away.

Ka-boom! Blinded by the bright blast of Obitoki's racer, Habba Kee crashed.

That left Sebulba and me.

I came up on his side. Sebulba might have had a lot of dirty tricks, but he didn't have a lot of imagination about using them. He knew flashing his side vents had worked once before on me. I had a feeling he'd try it again.

He did! My Podracer was forced onto the service ramp for a moment. Then I came right back. With a controlled thrust I ducked inside and took the lead!

Now Sebulba was behind me in second place! Boy, I wished I could have seen his face!

Crunk! The jarring jolt from behind caught me by surprise. Sebulba was taking out his frustrations by butting me. Now he was tight on my tail. He knew I wouldn't let him get past me, so instead he chose to crowd me and push, trying to send me out of control.

And that was a big problem, because it could work! It's hard enough to maneuver those turns at top speed without having someone bumping you from behind.

Sebulba kept pushing me and I kept fighting him off. My control board flickered. Something had been knocked loose and was shorting out.

Poo doo! It flickered again. I knew I'd have to switch to the auxiliary, but to do that meant backing off the RPMs. The electronics couldn't handle the jolt of switching at flat-out thrust.

It took less than a second to make the switch. But that was all Sebulba needed to retake the lead.

Last lap. Last turn. Last chance. A Nubian spacecraft was a lot to lose, and I had a feeling that was only the beginning of Qui-Gon's problems. I tried every move I knew to get past Sebulba. But either he'd gotten smarter during the race or he was just lucky, because he managed to keep me behind him.

Feel. Don't think. Trust your instincts. As we came out of the final turn, I put one last fake on him.

It worked! Suddenly we were side by side in the final stretch.

Crunk! Sebulba slammed his racer sideways into mine, trying to knock me off course.

Crunk! He did it again.

It took every bit of strength I had to keep my Podracer under control.

Crunk! Again! He was crazy! Smashing our racers together like this could hurt him as much as it could hurt me.

Crunk! This time when he slammed into me, we didn't bounce apart. I looked over the side and saw why. Our steering rods had gotten caught on each other!

In his Pod, Sebulba was frowning at me. If we crossed the finish line together, we'd tie. Neither of us wanted that. We both wanted to win.

I had to get loose!

Leaning as hard as I could on my racer's steering arm, I slammed my thruster bars back and forth, trying to break away from Sebulba's racer. Meanwhile we were screaming down the final stretch at top speed.

I pushed the steering arm harder.

Harder!

HARDER!

Snap! It broke!

Just before we burst apart, I caught a glimpse of incredible surprise on Sebulba's face. Then I was spinning wildly and pumping my stabilizers to straighten out.

A few moments later my racer limped through a cloud of black smoke and crossed the finish line. The smoke was coming from Sebulba's engines, which had exploded when his Podracer crashed into an ancient statue. I don't know how he managed to survive that crash, but he did.

Only he didn't win the Boonta Classic.

I did.

I slowed to a stop and just sat there in my racer, so tired that I couldn't even reach up to undo my straps. My face was wet with gritty sweat. My ears were filled with the hiss of the cooling turbines and the roar of the cheering crowd. The twin suns glared down out of the cloudless sky, glinting off the Radon-Ulzers. My race . . . my win . . . my dream . . .

Kitster was reaching into the Pod and undoing my straps. I looked up into his proud, smiling face. His lips moved but I couldn't hear his words over the roar. Hands were picking me up and the next thing I knew, I was being carried toward the royal box by a crowd of cheering fans.

I'd done it.

I'd won.

Sixth Entry
The Biggest Surprise

It wasn't until I got back to the hangar that I saw Mom, Qui-Gon, Padmé, and the others. Everyone congratulated me, and Padmé gave me a hug. Even Mom was proud of me. I guess my winning the Boonta Classic gave the Tatooine slaves hope. Maybe not that *they* could win the race. But that they could achieve whatever they wanted if they really worked at it.

Qui-Gon had already used our winnings to buy the parts he needed for his ship. Now he borrowed some eopies and a repulsor sled to carry the parts back to the desert. Jar Jar and Artoo-Detoo left for the ship on foot. As Padmé climbed onto one of the eopies, I wondered if I'd ever see her again. I wanted to ask her, but there were too many people around.

Mom and I went home. For the rest of the day I should have basked in the glory of winning the race. All the kids in the neighborhood came by to congratulate me. They wanted to play and talk, but I was distracted. I had a project I needed to finish — fast.

You see, I was sad that Padmé was leaving and I hadn't had a chance to say good-bye. I knew Qui-Gon would come back to return the eopies. When he did, I wanted to give him something to give to her. Something she would remember me by.

I had a piece of japor wood that I'd found in the desert and was saving. Japor was rare and valuable, and anything made of it was supposed to bring the wearer good luck. Now I started carving a pendant from it. My hope was that Padmé would wear it around her neck. . . .

I finished the pendant and went out to find a leather lace to hang it on. Everywhere I went, people waved and smiled. I felt funny. I'd never been a hero before.

Not everyone was happy about my win. Out of nowhere a Rodian named Wald appeared in front of me, blocking my path. Wald was usually a friend of mine. But one look at him and I knew he was no friend today.

Maybe he'd lost money on the race. Or maybe he just didn't like Humans. All I knew was that he wanted to fight because he said no Human could have won the Boonta Classic. Therefore, I must have cheated.

He got the fight he wanted.

But even as our fists flew, I wasn't thinking about him or the race. I was thinking about Padmé.

We were rolling on the ground, flailing at each other and kicking up dust when I felt a shadow loom over me.

Looking up, I saw Qui-Gon gazing down at me with a frown on his face. I quickly stood up and dusted myself off. The Jedi Knight asked what had happened. I told him how Wald had accused me of cheating.

He turned to Wald and asked him if he thought I'd cheated. To my surprise, even though I'd just pounded him halfway into a pulp, Wald nodded. He *still* thought I'd cheated!

Qui-Gon nodded knowingly and turned once again to me. He explained that fighting had not changed Wald's mind. I would have to be satisfied knowing the truth — that I didn't cheat — even if I couldn't convince everyone else.

I realized Qui-Gon was teaching me a lesson. I might have won the race, but all the fighting in the world wouldn't convince an enemy to take my side.

Qui-Gon and I went back to my house. When we got inside, he told me something I never expected to hear. It made me forget almost everything else. Winning the Boonta Classic was *nothing* compared to this.

The Jedi Knight said I was no longer a slave! *I was free!* It seemed impossible that Watto would give me up, but all Qui-Gon would say was that Watto had learned an important lesson about gambling.

Mom was thrilled for me. She said now I could make my dreams come true. Then she asked Qui-Gon if I was to become a Jedi.

A Jedi?!

I was completely shocked! But Qui-Gon didn't seem surprised by the question. Then I remembered the serious conversation I'd watched them have the day before. This *had* to be what they'd talked about!

But me, a Jedi Knight? That was always a dream. I never, ever dared to believe it could really come true.

Qui-Gon kneeled down so that we were face-to-face. He looked very serious and told me it was no coincidence that we'd met. He said that I was strong with the Force. But he warned me that I still might not be accepted by the Council. I wasn't exactly sure how the Council worked, but

I had a feeling it must have been made up of other Jedi Knights.

He also warned me that if I was accepted, there would be a long period of training. It would not be an easy life. He could have told me I'd have to shovel bantha poo for the rest of my days. It wouldn't have mattered if it meant being a Jedi.

Mom told me to hurry and get packed because I would have to go back to the ship with Qui-Gon and there wasn't much time. I turned and started toward my room. But then I thought of something that made me stop in my tracks.

I looked back at them. Mom and Qui-Gon shared a knowing look. And suddenly I knew this wasn't only good news after all.

Seventh Entry
A Difficult Decision

The bad news was that Mom couldn't come with us. Qui-Gon had tried to free her too, but Watto refused. Even the money from selling my Podracer wasn't enough.

Leave Mom on Tatooine? I couldn't do it. Even if it meant not becoming a Jedi. I didn't want to go without her. Coruscant was halfway across the galaxy — light-years away. It was too far. If I went there, there was a good chance I'd never see her again.

I tried to tell her, but she told me to listen to my feelings. I tried to pretend that my feelings wanted me to stay on Tatooine, but we both knew that wasn't true. In my heart, I wanted to be a Jedi more than anything in the world. Finally, I went to my room and quickly packed.

It was hard to leave. Kitster and some of my other friends were playing outside, and when they saw me come out with Qui-Gon and my bag, they knew something unusual was going on. I told Kitster I was free and going off planet. Of course, I couldn't tell him why. He told me everyone wanted me to stay because I was a hero. That made me feel a little bad.

Then he told me I was the best friend he'd ever had, and that made me feel good.

A little way down the street, Qui-Gon was waiting for me. I started toward him, but when I looked back I saw Mom standing in the doorway of our hovel. That was the only place I remembered living. And she was the only person in my family. I felt a lump in my throat and a big sadness inside me. I went back to her and told her I couldn't do it. I just couldn't go off and leave her.

Mom reminded me of the time I climbed the Great Dune to chase the banthas away before the hunters could shoot them. It was a broiling hot day and I never thought I'd make it to the top, but I knew I had to try. I even collapsed a couple of times. But somehow I'd made it.

And because of that, a small herd of banthas had lived.

Mom said this was one of those times when I had to surprise myself. I had to do something I didn't think I could do. Because, like saving those banthas, something good would come of it.

I had to let go.

When I asked her if I would ever see her again, she gazed back at me and nodded. I'll never forget what she said: "What does your heart tell you?"

It was strange, but right then my dream came back to me. I could see now how it might all indeed come true. I would come back. I would become a Jedi, then someday return and free all the slaves.

"Yes, I think so," I said.

Mom smiled and nodded. "Then we will see each other again."

Knowing that gave me the strength to go forward.

I joined Qui-Gon. We had to go to Watto's shop first. I would have preferred to never see my former master again, but there were forms to fill out that guaranteed my freedom. And the transmitter hidden in my body had to be deactivated.

Watto grumbled once or twice about how unfairly he felt he'd been treated, but when Qui-Gon shot him a stern look, he got quiet — fast.

Qui-Gon wanted me to hurry back to the ship, but there was one last stop I had to make before I left Tatooine. I had to go back to the market and find Jira.

I found her at her stand and told her I'd been freed and that I was going away. Then I gave her some of the credits from the sale of my Podracer and told her to get herself that cooling unit I'd promised her.

She gave me a hug and said she'd miss me.

I turned and started away with Qui-Gon. We hurried through the hot, sun-blasted streets of Mos Espa. I was surprised by the feeling of homesickness growing inside me. Miss *this* hot, barren place? I couldn't believe it. And yet I knew I would.

Suddenly Qui-Gon swung around. The glowing blade of his lightsaber sliced through something hovering in the air near us. I was amazed. I thought my fakes were good, but they were nothing compared to the way Qui-Gon reacted.

The thing he'd cut out of the air was about the size of a loaf of bread. Now sliced in two, its parts lay sparking and fizzing on the ground. Qui-Gon kneeled down and studied it carefully. I asked him what it was. A probe droid, he said, but unlike any he'd seen before.

He looked around quickly. The droid was a bad sign. A moment later we were running as fast as we could toward the ship.

We ran across the hot sands on the outskirts of Mos Espa. I wanted to ask Qui-Gon why we were running, but I was too busy trying to keep

up with him. Soon I could see the Nubian spacecraft ahead, standing on its landing struts. She was a beauty. Sleek with swept-back wings, she was as fine as any spacecraft I'd ever seen.

Without warning Qui-Gon wheeled around and yelled at me to drop. I did what I was told, and not a second too soon. A dark-cloaked figure on a speeder bike shot over me. If I'd been standing I would have been skewered. In a flash the dark figure jumped to the ground and ignited a lightsaber. A split second later he and Qui-Gon were exchanging earthshaking lightsaber blows.

Even the worst Podrace was less scary and dangerous than this. I didn't know who that dark warrior was, but he attacked Qui-Gon so viciously that the Jedi Knight could barely fend off the blows.

This warrior was strange and evil-looking. Shaped like a Human's, his face was covered with red and black markings. Short, pointed horns grew out of his head.

Qui-Gon looked as if he was in trouble, but I knew there was no way I could help. He yelled at me to go to the ship and tell the others to take off.

That I could do. I pushed myself off the sand and started to run. Right up the boarding ramp and through the Nubian's hatch. Padmé and a man in a captain's uniform were inside. I blurted out what was going on and what Qui-Gon had said.

They hurried away toward the flight deck. I stayed near the hatch and watched the battle outside. Not that I could see much. Just the cloud of dust and the brilliant flashes of the lightsabers.

As terrifying as it was, it also gave me a moment to wonder. I'd heard from the spacers who passed through Mos Espa that Jedi were the most powerful fighters in the galaxy. But that thing in the dark cloak seemed at least as strong as Qui-Gon. What could it possibly be?

With a slight jolt, the Naboo spacecraft lifted off the ground. For a second I thought we were going to take off without Qui-Gon. But the ship rose only a few meters and then started to move . . . straight toward the battle.

The ship turned slightly and I tried to watch the battle through the window. Meanwhile, the pilot was steering the ship toward them. The hatch was still open. I quickly understood the plan. They weren't leaving Qui-Gon — they were going to pick him up! I just hoped they'd figured out how to do it without picking up that dark warrior, too.

We were higher now. Maybe a half dozen meters from the ground. Suddenly Qui-Gon appeared out of the cloud of chaos beneath us! He'd jumped up to the ramp!

But an instant later, the dark warrior appeared on the ramp, too!

Qui-Gon swung his lightsaber as hard as he could at his attacker.

Crack! The whole ship shuddered from the impact.

I watched in amazement as the warrior fell back to the ground. He landed on his feet and glared up at us with the most evil yellow eyes I'd ever seen. Just the sight of them made me shiver.

The hatch snapped shut. I barely had time to grab a handhold before the ship rocketed upward.

I caught my breath and watched the sky change. Below us, Mos Espa was no larger than a sandbox and getting smaller all the time.

Then the sky turned from blue to black and I was staring down at a bare, sand-colored planet. Beyond it glowed my familiar twin suns. Everywhere else, the sky was awash with sparkling stars.

For the first time in my life, I was in space.

Eighth Entry
The Queen

I could have stayed at that window staring out at the stars for a long time. But I was worried about Qui-Gon. The Jedi Knight had collapsed on the floor inside the hatch. Artoo-Detoo was already there. A young man I hadn't seen before was there, too. One look at his clothes and lightsaber and I knew he was also a Jedi.

Qui-Gon was breathing hard. His face was wet with sweat and streaked with dust and dirt. I asked if he was all right and he said he thought so, but I could see that he was shaken. The dark warrior had come as a complete surprise.

The younger Jedi asked Qui-Gon what he thought the warrior was. Qui-Gon said he wasn't sure, but that the warrior was well trained in the Jedi arts.

That puzzled me. How could you be well trained in the Jedi arts and not be a Jedi? But even more confusing was what Qui-Gon said next — that he thought the warrior had come after the Queen.

I asked Qui-Gon if he thought the dark warrior would follow our ship. He answered that we would be safe once we entered hyperspace, but that he had no doubt the warrior knew our final destination.

The thought of meeting up with the dark warrior again made me shiver. I asked what we could do about him.

Before Qui-Gon could answer, the other Jedi gave me a puzzled look.

"Anakin Skywalker, meet Obi-Wan Kenobi," Qui-Gon said.

I held out my hand to shake his.

But when we shook, the new Jedi stared at me with one eyebrow raised.

I didn't think he liked me.

We were in hyperspace. The parts Qui-Gon had purchased from Watto had done the trick and we were now moving faster than the speed of light. Hyperspace is a silent vacuum, and the only sounds in the ship were the hums of the navigational and life-support systems. Obi-Wan Kenobi had taken Qui-Gon to his quarters to rest after his battle.

Obi-Wan was shorter than Qui-Gon. Except for the braided pigtail that hung over his right shoulder and a small ponytail, he had short hair. I figured that he was an apprentice to the older Jedi.

With Qui-Gon in another part of the ship, I was alone, and cold.

In fact, I was shivering. The Naboo spacecraft was freezing.

I sat down in a corner and pulled my knees under my chin to try and stay warm. Now that it was quiet, I felt very lonely. I'd left my home with strangers to go to a place on the other side of the galaxy. Coruscant was so far away that I might never be able to go home. I knew Qui-Gon wanted to take care of me, but after his battle with the dark warrior he had his own problems. It was still hard to believe that there were warriors in the galaxy who might be equal to, or even greater than, a Jedi Knight. But now I knew there were. And if something happened to Qui-Gon, who would present me to the Council? Who would train me in the ways of the Jedi?

Who would believe that I even had what it took to become a Jedi?

I felt someone watching me and looked up. It was Padmé. She asked if I was cold and I admitted that I was. She gave me her jacket and teased me about being from a hot planet like

Tatooine. She said space was cold. I told her that I'd already figured that out.

Padmé looked worried, so I asked her what was wrong. She told me the Queen had problems. The people on Naboo were suffering. Some were even dying.

I was sitting there wishing I had a way to cheer her up when I remembered the japor pendant. I took it out of my pocket and gave it to her. I told her that it would always remind her of me and bring her good luck.

I have to admit that I was more than a little nervous. Not only was Padmé beautiful, but I could tell by her delicate clothes and her gentle manner that she was used to very fine things. I wasn't sure how she'd feel about wearing a wooden pendant carved by a boy.

But Padmé smiled and immediately put it on. She said she loved it. And she said she wouldn't need anything to remind her of me. She promised she would never forget me.

I was in the cockpit of the spaceship when the pilot brought us out of hyperspace. We were at the inner core of the galaxy. The sky was dense with brightly twinkling stars and systems.

Directly below us was Coruscant, the capital of the Galactic Republic. I'd dreamed of visiting Coruscant, but it was even better than I'd imagined. The entire planet was covered by a huge sprawling city with every imaginable size and shape building. Some were so tall their metallic spires pierced the clouds.

We started to drop down toward the planet. The endless city had canyons like Tatooine, but they were the canyons between buildings. The airspace was clogged with hundreds of different vehicles — from small messenger speeders to huge, slow-moving transports.

We moved into a traffic lane and then onto a floating landing platform. Qui-Gon and Obi-Wan Kenobi joined Jar Jar and me near the hatch.

An important-looking group of people was waiting on the landing platform. Before the hatch opened, Qui-Gon instructed Jar Jar and me on how to bow and show respect. He told us to stay out of the way and take our cues from him and Obi-Wan.

When the hatch opened, we did as we were told and moved off to the edge of the platform to get a closer look at the huge city surrounding us. I think Jar Jar was even more amazed than I was. He just stared and stared with his big frog eyes.

Meanwhile, I kept one eye on what was happening behind us. I was glad I did or I would have missed what came next. Several royal guards stepped down the ramp, *and then came Queen Amidala!*

I could hardly believe I was standing so close to royalty. It was obvious that she was powerful. You could tell by her powdery-white face, and black-and-gold royal garb. On her head was a headpiece made of large black feathers. The important men I'd just bowed to were now bowing to her!

After the Queen came three handmaidens wearing fiery-colored cloaks. Padmé was one of them.

Padmé gave me a quick smile while the Queen spoke in a hushed voice to the important-looking men who'd come to greet her. You could see that this wasn't just a friendly welcoming party. Their faces were serious and their whispering sounded urgent.

Then the Queen and her guards and handmaidens moved off toward a waiting air shuttle.

She motioned for us to follow.

Jar Jar and I were taken to a large building. We were sent to a waiting room and told to stay put. Padmé had to go somewhere, and I watched through a doorway as Queen Amidala sat on a throne and had more meetings with important-looking men in uniforms. Their faces were very grim and there was a lot of head shaking.

Something was seriously wrong. From the bits and pieces I was able to overhear on the air shuttle, I knew that a group called the Trade Federation had surrounded the planet Naboo with huge battleships. No supplies were being allowed in or out of Naboo, and that was why the Queen's people were suffering.

But what did that have to do with the dark warrior? That was the part I still didn't understand. He was only one being. I decided that he might have been part of the problem, but there had to be more to it. Something even more serious was happening.

Jar Jar and I waited. I felt bad for him because he looked as lonely and lost as me. At least I had a reason for coming to Coruscant. Qui-Gon had brought me to see if I could become a Jedi. Jar Jar seemed to be here because he had no place else to go.

I asked him why he wasn't with his people. In his strange language, Jar Jar explained he had been banished for wrecking his leader's favorite vehicle. The rest had all happened by accident. He'd been sitting in a Naboo swamp one day enjoying a meal when he got caught in an invasion! He was saved by Qui-Gon, and had been with the Jedi Knight ever since.

A messenger arrived saying that in a little while I would be picked up by taxi and taken to the Jedi

Temple. Qui-Gon's words came back to me. I remembered that if I was accepted for Jedi training, I would be busy for a long time. I realized this might be my last chance to see Padmé. I wanted to find her.

I left the waiting room and started down a hall. Of course, I had no idea where anything was, or where I might find Padmé. So I watched for clues. Finally I found what I was looking for. A handmaiden came past me carrying a bowl of fruit. There was a chance she was taking it to the Queen's quarters, where I hoped to find Padmé.

The handmaiden turned down several halls and then went through a door watched over by two guards. That looked promising, but I hesitated anyway. I felt nervous. I didn't know what the guards would do when they saw me. What if this was a restricted area and I wasn't supposed to be in the hall?

It took more courage to walk down that hall and face those guards than it did to get in my Pod and race against Sebulba. But I did it. For Padmé.

Lucky for me, the guards were friendly. I guess being nine years old has its advantages. I told them I was looking for Padmé. One of them spoke into a comlink and then told me to go through the door they were guarding.

I went into a small room. At the other end a

door was open and I could see into a larger room. Another of the Queen's handmaidens greeted me. I had seen her come off the ship with Padmé. I didn't know her name, but she knew mine. From the smile on her face I could see that she already knew why I had come.

I was disappointed when she told me Padmé wasn't there. I expected to leave then, but suddenly a voice called from the other room, asking who it was. The handmaiden called back that it was Anakin Skywalker, here to see Padmé.

What happened next took me by complete surprise: Queen Amidala herself came to the doorway. Remembering Qui-Gon's instructions, I instantly bowed, then peeked up at her.

The Queen was now wearing a fancy gown and a fan-shaped crown of beads and tassels. A single red mark had been painted on each of her cheeks. She said she'd sent Padmé on an errand.

I apologized for bothering her and explained that I had been called to the Jedi Temple where I hoped to start my training. I was worried that I might not see Padmé again. I had come to say good-bye.

The Queen said she would give Padmé my message. Padmé must have told her about me because the Queen said she was sure Padmé's heart would go with me.

I felt bad that I wouldn't get to see Padmé. But I thanked the Queen, and left to find the cab that would take me to the Jedi Temple.

Where my future was to be decided.

Ninth Entry
The Future Is Uncertain

Even on the vast city-planet of Coruscant, you could spot the Jedi Temple right away. Not only was it huge, its flat-topped pyramid shape was unlike any other building around it.

Once again I had to wait in a room outside a main chamber. And again it was cold. Unlike the dual star system Tatooine revolved around, Coruscant circled a single star.

As I waited in the room, I noticed something written above the door:

There is no emotion; there is peace.
There is no ignorance; there is knowledge.
There is no passion; there is serenity.
There is no death; there is the Force.

The words were stark and bare. All of a sudden I felt a little afraid.

Emotion? Up till now, pretty much all of my life had involved emotions like anger, and fear, and even hatred. How could you grow up a slave on Tatooine and *not* know those emotions?

Ignorance? I didn't have to spend much time with learned people like Qui-Gon and Padmé to realize that I had grown up surrounded by ignorance. Slave children received no schooling or training. What we learned, we learned on our own. And even though my mother taught me everything she knew, I realize now how much I still have to learn.

Death? Even at my young age, I had seen plenty of it.

It was sunset when Qui-Gon finally came for me. He apologized for making me wait so long and explained that the Council had had several unusually serious matters to deal with that day. I didn't ask what those matters were. Qui-Gon would have told me if he'd wanted me to know. But I had a feeling the dark warrior was one of them.

Qui-Gon led me into the Council chamber. The room was circular, its ceiling domed, its walls lined with large windows looking out upon the city. I found myself standing with Qui-Gon and Obi-Wan, surrounded by the twelve members of the

Jedi Council. Men, women, Humans, and other beings, they were seated in a circle. But the strangest was the one who appeared to be the most important. He was as unlike a Jedi as I could have imagined.

They called him Yoda and he was no bigger than a Jawa. But unlike a Jawa, whose face is always hidden by a hood, Yoda's almost bare, wrinkled head was uncovered. His complexion was light green. He had a broad forehead, bulging eyes, and long, pointed ears that stretched away from either side of his skull. Had I come across him on the streets of Tatooine, I probably would not have looked twice. But I admit I was surprised to find such a creature at the head of the Jedi Council.

I wish I could say that I was greeted with welcoming smiles and open arms. But the Jedi Council gave me grave looks. Only Yoda's face revealed an open, warm expression.

In a low, gravelly voice, Yoda told me that I should relax and empty my mind. I would be asked some questions. Everyone went silent. Another important-looking Jedi, whose name was Mace Windu, picked up a small viewing screen, but I couldn't tell what was on it.

He asked what I saw in my mind and I told him: a Republic Cruiser. A Rodian cup. A Hutt speeder. . . .

Mace Windu nodded and turned off the viewing screen. Yoda asked me how I felt and I told him the truth. I felt cold. Then he asked me if I was afraid and I said I wasn't.

Mace Windu asked if I was afraid to give up my life.

I suppose I hesitated there for a moment. I thought of Mom. Of how I missed her and how unhappy she'd be if I died.

Then I realized what I'd done. But it was too late. They'd seen my thoughts. They knew I missed Mom. I think it made me a little mad. They'd read my thoughts so clearly and they knew something about me that I didn't want them to. When Yoda asked if I was afraid to lose her, I snapped and asked what that had to do with anything.

"Everything," Yoda calmly replied. "Fear is the path to the dark side . . . fear leads to anger . . . anger leads to hate . . . hate leads to suffering."

I panicked. I was failing the test! And that made me *really* mad. To come this close to my dream . . . I couldn't fail. I just couldn't! I insisted that I wasn't afraid.

The Council members glanced at Yoda, who nodded knowingly.

"A Jedi must have the deepest commitment, the most serious mind," he said slowly. "I sense much fear in you."

I fought back the impulse to argue. Instead I knew I had to answer calmly and firmly. And without anger. I remembered what was written outside — *there is no passion; there is serenity.*

"I am not afraid," I said softly.

The faces of the other Jedi were blank. I couldn't tell if they believed me. But Yoda said we could continue. . . .

More questions followed. I tried my best to answer them honestly and not let my emotions get in the way.

When the questioning ended, Qui-Gon, Obi-Wan, and I left the room and waited outside. Neither of the two Jedi standing with me revealed very much. I sensed that Qui-Gon was eager and hopeful. Oddly, Obi-Wan's feeling seemed to be the exact opposite. From him I sensed impatience, and even annoyance that he had to be there with Qui-Gon and me. I was pretty sure he didn't like me.

Meanwhile, the Council members spoke quietly. Recalling how easily Yoda and the others had read my thoughts, I wondered if they were now sharing their own thoughts on my future. I might have been able to control my thoughts, but I couldn't control my heart. It was pounding as hard as if I were in the final stretch of a Podrace.

Finally, we were called back into the Council

chamber. Yoda and the other Jedi spoke. They said my body cells contained a high concentration of something called *midi-chlorians* and that the Force was strong with me.

Qui-Gon seemed glad. He assumed that meant they agreed with him and that I was to be trained!

But his words were met by an uncomfortable silence.

No, said Mace Windu. I would not be trained.

I couldn't stop the tears that suddenly flooded into my eyes. I'd come all this way! They said the Force was strong in me. How could they do this?

Qui-Gon seemed stunned and asked the Jedi Council's reason. Mace Windu explained that I was too old to begin the training.

Too *old?* I'm only nine! It sounded crazy, but then I remembered what an old spacer had once told me. He knew about the Jedi and had even flown with them into battle once long ago. I remembered now that he'd said that Jedi were almost always identified before they turned one year old.

Then Mace Windu added that the Council sensed that there was too much anger inside me.

I wanted to tell them that they were wrong. If there was anger in me I could control it. I could rise above it! But I knew I had to appear calm. I couldn't let them know I was feeling angry.

Qui-Gon argued some more. He refused to accept the Council's decision. I was the chosen one, he said, and they had to accept that.

The *chosen* one?

Even Obi-Wan reacted to those words, staring with surprise at Qui-Gon and then at me.

Yoda would only say that my future was clouded. They couldn't be sure.

I didn't understand. What did they mean by chosen one? Why did I come all this way and leave the only life I knew if I couldn't become a Jedi?

Qui-Gon fought and fought. He said that even if the Council disagreed he would train me as his own Padawan Learner.

Obi-Wan looked shocked. His jaw dropped and for a second I thought he would challenge Qui-Gon. But then he caught himself. I may have imagined it, but for a split second I thought he narrowed his eyes at me before turning to face the Council.

From the looks on the faces of the Council members, I knew that Qui-Gon had gone too far. Yoda said it was impossible for Qui-Gon to take me as an apprentice as long as he already had one. Qui-Gon told the Council that Obi-Wan was ready.

Beside him the younger Jedi nodded and said he was ready to face the trials of becoming a Jedi Knight.

Again, the faces of the Council said that they disagreed. Yoda said he doubted that Obi-Wan was ready, even though Qui-Gon said he had taught the younger Jedi all he could.

Suddenly the discussion stopped. Mace Windu informed the Council that the decision on my future would have to wait. The Senate was voting for a new Supreme Chancellor. Queen Amidala was returning to her home on planet Naboo. This would widen the confrontation with the Trade Federation.

Yoda added that it would also draw out the Queen's attacker. Despite all my mixed-up feelings, I was now certain that Yoda was speaking of the dark warrior. I was scared for the Queen, but I admit I thought of Padmé first. Since she attended the Queen, her life would also be in danger.

The councilors spoke in serious tones. One of them said the events were moving too fast. They were really worried. Mace Windu told Qui-Gon and Obi-Wan to go with the Queen to Naboo. He wanted them to protect the Queen and discover the identity of the dark warrior.

And then I heard a word I had only heard once before. A thing I doubted truly existed.

Until now.

Tenth Entry
Past and Future

As I've said before, all manner of strange and frightening voyagers passed through Tatooine. This included some pretty weird old droids.

One day, about a year before Qui-Gon's ship landed on Tatooine, I was looking for something in Watto's junk heap when I came across an old war droid. This unit was *really* ancient. It was covered with rusty armor plating and even had a fuse box — something I'd only heard about.

Being curious about old technologies, I dragged it behind the shop and waited until Watto was gone. Then I hooked it up to a universal power source, just to see what would happen. As I suspected, the unit was frozen. Most of its joints had dried up long ago.

But its electronics were still intact and it

seemed to have a working holoprojector. I knew Watto would want a working holoprojector, no matter how old it was. He could always peddle it off to some local mechanic trying to build his own droid.

I was in the middle of testing the projector when a holograph burst on. It showed some sort of ancient battle, but the visual projection was really bad. I was disappointed. Maybe the projector wasn't worth salvaging after all.

I was just about to give up when the audio came on. It, too, was very poor quality, and mostly static. But I could hear screams and grunts and panicked shouts. Something about the Sith this and the Sith that. I couldn't really get a handle on what was going on. All I could tell was that whatever these Sith things were, they were very, very bad.

I ran the sequence over and over again, trying to get a look at this Sith thing and figure out what could possibly be so terrible about it.

While the screams of terror chilled me, I was a little bit fascinated and curious. But then the holoprojector stopped working.

I couldn't get those vague sounds and images out of my mind. On my way home that day I passed some of the cantinas that lined the marketplace. Sitting outside was a deep-space pilot I sometimes saw around. According to my friends, he'd landed on Tatooine with no fuel or money and seemed content to spend the rest of his days sitting in the shade out of the twin suns, telling anyone who would listen stories about his life and travels. He was the one who'd first told me about the angels on the moons of lego.

The old spacer waved at me, and I went over to chat. I knew he was the real thing because of the Old Republic fighter corps insignia on his tunic. After a few moments I asked him if he'd ever heard of a Sith. To be honest, I expected him to chuckle and shake his head.

Instead, the old spacer turned pale. His eyes widened and his jaw dropped. He began looking around with a panicked expression. Where had I heard of them? he wanted to know. Were they back? Were they here on Tatooine?

It took a couple of minutes to explain that I'd simply seen an old holograph. A couple of minutes more passed before he calmed down enough to tell me the story.

He said the Sith had come into being thousands of years ago. They were founded by a rogue Jedi Knight who believed that the real Force lay not in the light, but in the dark. He recruited others and trained them in the art of battle. For a time the Sith Lords had been the most fearsome warriors in the galaxy. Fiercer even than the Jedi. Because unlike the Jedi, the Sith were evil and loved war, not peace.

The good news was that their evil eventually turned inward and they began to battle each other. Soon all but a few had been destroyed, and the Jedi were able to get rid of the rest.

Or so it was said. Some people thought that one Sith Lord had survived in secret. Now and then someone would report seeing him, but none of the rumors had ever been proven.

Until now, here in the Jedi Council chamber. I heard the word Sith spoken again. And learned that this was what Qui-Gon thought the dark warrior was.

If Queen Amidala was being stalked by a Sith Lord, I knew she was *really* in danger! I was so preoccupied with the thought that I barely heard Yoda tell the Jedi Council that my fate as a Jedi would be decided at another time.

Qui-Gon said I would have to stay with him, since I had nowhere else to go. Yoda and the others agreed, but they warned Qui-Gon that while I was to accompany him, I was not to be trained.

When I left the Jedi Council my head was spinning. So much had happened and so many different things had been discussed! I didn't know what to think. There was the doubt over my future as a Jedi. And Obi-Wan's obvious displeasure with me. But also the threat to the Queen and the danger Padmé must be facing. . . .

And now I was to go with Qui-Gon and Obi-Wan to the planet of Naboo, where they would attempt to protect the Queen against the mysterious and evil Sith Lord. I would be lying if I said I wasn't frightened. But I was also excited to go.

To me, Coruscant had become a place where everyone treated me like a kid. I felt helpless there. I could only hope that it would be different on Naboo.

Coruscant at night is as amazing as it is by day. The whole planet is lit by the lights of its single, sprawling city. I stood on the windy landing platform with Qui-Gon, Obi-Wan, and Artoo-Deetoo. Ever since the Council meeting, the two Jedi had been edgy and uncomfortable with each other. Now, on the platform, their feelings finally came out. I could see the strained looks on their faces as they spoke, but their words were whisked away with the wind.

I wished I could hear what they were saying. Then I remembered how, in the Jedi Temple, they told me to relax and open my mind, and how I'd been able to picture the images from Mace Windu's viewing screen when I did.

I tried to do the same now. The Jedi were probably skilled at masking their thoughts if they suspected someone was listening. But I doubted they would expect that from me. And so I "listened" and learned that Obi-Wan thought the Council would be right in denying me Jedi training. He said the whole Council sensed that I was dangerous.

Dangerous? I had to stop myself from arguing. How could Obi-Wan say I was dangerous? He didn't even *know* me! But that, I realized, was the whole point. Because Obi-Wan didn't know me, he couldn't be arguing about me personally. It was the *idea* of me — already nine years old, but with very high midi-chlorians — that he was talking about.

I was very glad when Qui-Gon said that while my fate might be uncertain, I was not dangerous. He reminded Obi-Wan that the Council had not made their final decision.

Then he told the younger Jedi to go on board the Naboo spacecraft. Obi-Wan went up the boarding ramp reluctantly.

I was glad he left because I wanted the chance to tell Qui-Gon what I was thinking. That even though I was eager to go to Naboo, maybe I shouldn't. Because of the more serious problems they were facing — the Trade Federation blockade and the threat of the Sith Lord — I didn't want to be in the way.

Qui-Gon assured me that I wouldn't be a

bother. He said he would not go against the Council by training me, but that didn't mean I couldn't watch him and learn. Above all, I was to stay close to him, because that way I would be safe.

It seemed he was waiting for the Queen and in no rush to board the ship, so I asked him about something else that was bothering me. What were midi-chlorians?

Qui-Gon explained that they were microscopic life-forms that lived in all body cells and communicated with the Force. In a way, the two life-forms depended on each other. The midi-chlorians needed us in order to live and we needed them in order to know the Force. He said it was the midi-chlorians that told us the will of the Force and that when I learned to quiet my mind, I would be able to hear them.

From my experience just a few moments before on the landing platform, I was beginning to have a sense of what he meant. I wanted to ask him more, but we were interrupted by the arrival of an air transport carrying the Queen.

Qui-Gon greeted Amidala, who seemed glad to see him. I overheard the Queen say that she was worried that the Trade Federation wanted to destroy her. The Jedi Knight promised her that wouldn't happen.

The Queen had a small group with her, but before I could look for Padmé, Jar Jar burst out of the transport and hugged me. All he could talk about was how glad he was to be going home. By the time I managed to get out of his grasp, the Queen and her handmaidens had gone on board.

Later, on the ship, I went looking for Padmé and somehow found myself in the ship's control center. This was by far the most advanced cockpit I'd ever seen. I wasn't sure how the pilot, Ric Olié, would feel about me hanging around, but he didn't mind at all. In fact, he went over all the controls with me.

The strange thing was that while the Nubian ship had many more controls than any ship I'd seen in Watto's junkyard, the basics were the same. I could identify the thrusters, stabilizers, and repulsors. I don't think Ric Olié would have been so impressed with my knowledge if he'd known how many junked cockpits I'd sat in.

I didn't see Padmé until the very end of the flight. We'd entered the Naboo atmosphere and were starting to land. When I came out of the hydrolift, the Queen and her people were in the main hold waiting to disembark.

I saw Padmé. From the way she carried herself, I could see that she was prepared to fight. I sensed that she was as well trained in warfare as in attending to the Queen.

That's when my dream came back to me. Once

again I saw Padmé leading that huge army, and I knew that she could do it.

Padmé seemed surprised to see me. But pleased, too. She told me the Queen had given her my message back on Coruscant. Then she asked what had happened at the Jedi Temple.

I told her the bad news. It appeared that the Council might not allow me to be trained as a Jedi. I could tell she was disappointed. And she looked worried, too. I asked her what was wrong and she said that the Queen had decided that her people had to go to war against the Trade Federation. I told Padmé that I might not be a Jedi, but that didn't mean I couldn't help.

Padmé smiled at me. It was a sad smile.

The ship landed with a slight jolt. When the hatch opened, I expected to see a landing pad and some sort of city, but I was in for a surprise.

Because all I saw was a swamp.

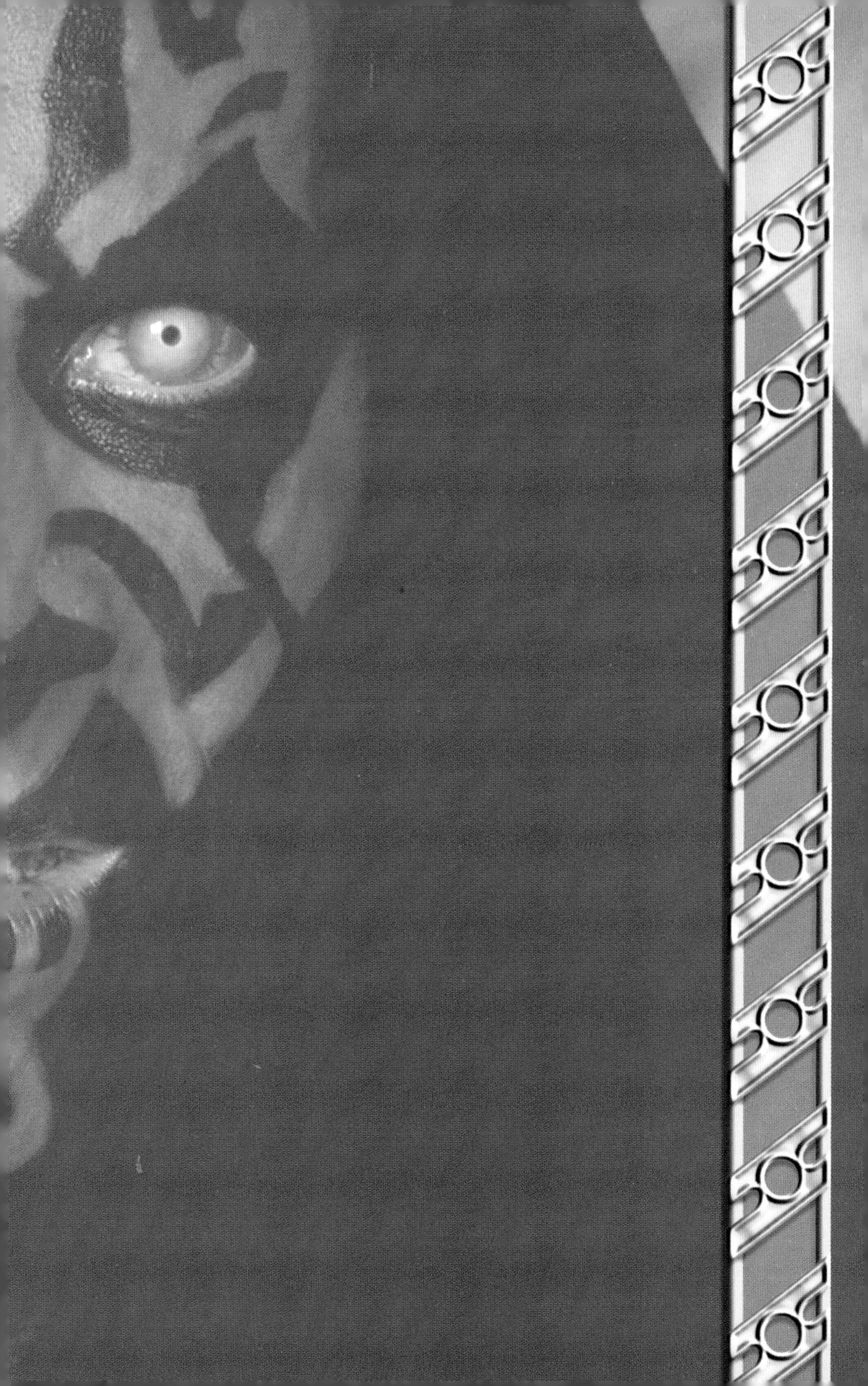

Eleventh Entry
Another Surprise

For a kid who grew up on the dry planet of Tatooine, seeing a lake for the first time was even more amazing than seeing the Queen. I couldn't believe that there were places where water actually lay on the ground without being instantly evaporated!

I looked around in shock. Here plants could grow wild and out in the open, not in some carefully managed subterranean farm.

Here it was so moist that you could actually feel the dampness on your skin and breathe the heaviness of the water vapor in the air!

Clouds blanketed the sky above and the mist hanging over the lake was the gray of twilight. Surrounding the lake was a swamp. In the distance I could see vast, grassy hills. All in all, this seemed an even stranger sight than the vast city-world of Coruscant.

Suddenly I felt homesick and alone. Why couldn't Mom be here to see this? And what about Kitster? Mom would look around in wonder. Kitster and I would be running around like crazy, touching the plants and splashing in the lake.

The lake may have been a strange and exotic place to me, but to Jar Jar it was home. With a giant splash he disappeared into the water. Someone said Jar Jar was Gungan. Gungans lived in a city deep below the surface. It seemed the Gungans and the Queen's people had never been friendly. But now Jar Jar was going on behalf of the Queen to plead for help in the battle she was about to face.

It wasn't long before Jar Jar returned to the surface. With lake water dripping off his ears and head, he gave us the bad news. He'd gone to the city, but it was deserted. I saw the worry in the faces around me. Obi-Wan feared that the Gungans had already been wiped out by the Trade Federation forces, but Jar Jar said it was more likely that his people had gone into hiding.

Jar Jar thought he knew where they were and began to lead us through the swamp. As we followed in a line behind him I kept my eyes on Padmé and Qui-Gon. I would have been glad to speak to either of them, but both seemed lost in thought.

Meanwhile, I could tell by the grumbling around me that not everyone believed that Jar Jar knew where he was going. After all, this was the creature who seemed incapable of staying out of trouble no matter where he went.

It wasn't long before he stopped, sniffed the air, and said we'd arrived. I looked around, but to me it still looked like a swamp. Jar Jar made some strange chattering sounds and suddenly, out of the dense green undergrowth, half a dozen Gungans appeared wearing uniforms and riding two-legged creatures I later learned were named kaadu.

They were armed with spearlike weapons that looked like long stun guns or electropoles. I assumed they were on patrol. And they didn't look pleased to find Jar Jar. I was starting to wonder if anyone was ever pleased to run into him. Even worse, when Jar Jar explained that we were there to speak to the boss of the Gungans, the leader of the patrol rolled his eyes and warned him that if we went to the boss Gungan, we would all be in serious trouble.

But Jar Jar insisted, and the leader of the patrol reluctantly agreed to lead us onward.

We followed the patrol leader to a place of ancient gray stone ruins, partly covered by green vines and brush. Jar Jar said this was a secret, sacred place for the Gungans. I looked around, amazed, as we passed groups of Gungans. They stared at us with their big eyes. Jar Jar whispered that they were refugees seeking shelter. They had been driven from their city at the bottom of the swamp by the forces of the Trade Federation.

We came to the remains of a huge stone temple that was covered with vines and moss. All that was left of it was crumbling columns and steps. Everywhere you looked were giant Gungan heads carved out of stone. Again, I wished Mom was there. It was all so strange and different.

We stopped before a heavy, sour-looking Gungan seated on a stone. Jar Jar whispered that this was Boss Nass, the chief Gungan. When Boss Nass saw Jar Jar and the rest of us, his broad forehead wrinkled, and his mouth frowned. After all, he was the guy who had banished Jar Jar.

Even when Queen Amidala stepped forward to say that we'd come in peace, Boss Nass shook his head. He warned Jar Jar that he'd made a mistake by bringing us to him, and that he was considering putting us all to death.

In a flash we were surrounded by Gungan guards. They lowered their electropoles at us. I heard the sharp intake of breath among those with the Queen. Realizing we were outnumbered, the Queen's guards looked around nervously. For a moment I went stiff, wondering if I'd come all this way just to die. But I was surprised to see Qui-Gon and Obi-Wan watching calmly, seemingly unbothered by the threat. If they weren't worried, I knew I could relax.

The biggest surprise was still to come. Queen Amidala began to say something about forming an alliance with the Gungans. But Padmé stepped forward, cutting her Queen short.

When the Gungan chief asked who she was, Padmé said she was the Queen!

For a moment I didn't understand what was happening. Padmé, the *Queen?* It didn't make sense.

But then she explained that the girl dressed as the Queen was actually one of her handmaidens. They had traded places for protection.

I'm glad Padmé wasn't looking in my direction because she would have seen my mouth hanging wide open!

I didn't know what to think! Ever since the day Padmé and Qui-Gon stepped into Watto's shop, my life had been changing in ways I would have never dared to imagine.

In some strange and secret way, I was connected to the Queen! That made me feel sort of important. It made me wonder.

Who *was* I?

Who was I destined to become?

Padmé went on to explain to Boss Nass why she had come. It was pretty obvious that even though the Naboo people and the Gungans had lived together on this planet for a long time in peace, they weren't exactly friendly.

Now, Padmé explained, they were both threatened by the Trade Federation. Unless the two groups banded together, they would both be destroyed.

Boss Nass listened to her with a frown on his face. You could see that he wasn't sure he believed her.

Suddenly Padmé dropped to her knees before the Gungan chief. She begged him. She said the Naboo people were his humble servants and their fate was in his hands.

From the gasps of her handmaidens and the Naboo guards, I knew that this was the last thing they had expected her to do. But then, slowly, the guards bowed, too. And then the handmaidens and the Jedi.

Boss Nass began to laugh. He seemed very pleased. He'd felt the Naboo people had thought they were better than his swamp-dwelling Gungans. Having the Naboo Queen on her knees begging him finally equaled things out.

He was starting to think that maybe the Gungans and Naboos might be allies after all. Once again I saw Padmé in a new light. Not only was she brave, she was also a skilled leader.

To me, she was even more than an angel.

After Boss Nass accepted the Queen's plea, he and his generals began to form a plan with Padmé and the Jedi Knights. I was still having trouble believing that Padmé was the real Naboo Queen. How could I call her Amidala? She would always be Padmé to me. She would always be that person I first felt a special connection to.

I wanted to talk to her in private, but she was busy saving her planet.

The leader of the Naboo guards and some of his men were sent to scout the activities of the Trade Federation troops. A Gungan sentry was stationed high up in the ancient temple to watch for their return.

When the lookout yelled that the guards were coming back, I let Padmé and the others know. Everyone was eager to hear what was happening between the Naboo people and the Trade Federation troops.

The news was bad. Most of the Naboo people had been thrown into prison camps. There was a small resistance movement made up of Naboo police officers and palace guards. But it was insignificant compared to the size of the Federation forces. They had a droid army that was larger than Padmé's advisors had expected.

From the grim expressions around me, I began to understand what we were up against. We would be totally outnumbered in battle. What could I do to help?

Then I heard some of what Padmé and the others had been planning. The Gungan troops would go to battle against the Federation droid army. It was doubtful that they could actually defeat the army, but hopefully they could draw them away from the city.

Meanwhile, a handful of Naboo troops would get into the city through secret passageways. They would attempt to enter the Royal Palace and capture the Trade Federation viceroy. He was the leader, and without him, the Trade Federation wouldn't know what to do.

Qui-Gon warned Padmé that the Trade Federation viceroy would be well protected and difficult to capture. He was also worried about the Gungan battle with the Trade Federation droids. Even though it was nothing more than a diversion, he feared that many Gungans might be killed.

Boss Nass bravely insisted that his people were ready to do their part to save the planet. Padmé pointed out that the enemy troops were controlled from a Trade Federation command center orbiting the planet. While entering Naboo airspace earlier, they had spotted a lone Trade Federation battleship: the Droid Control Ship. Part of the plan would be to also send Naboo fighter pilots to knock out the Control Ship. Then the droids on the surface would be helpless.

Qui-Gon agreed that it was a good plan, but again warned that it would not be easy. The Trade Federation Droid Control Ship was undoubtedly protected by deflector shields. If the Naboo pilots were unable to get through those shields, they wouldn't be able to disable the droid army below.

Then Obi-Wan pointed out an even greater danger. Everything depended on capturing the Trade Federation viceroy. If their plan failed and he escaped, he would no doubt return with an even bigger droid army — one that the meager Naboo and Gungan forces would have no hope of defeating.

Padmé nodded slowly and said she was aware of that risk. That was why the plan must not fail. The fate of all the beings on Naboo depended on capturing the viceroy.

With a risky plan and a thin thread of hope, we were going to war.

Twelfth Entry
A Greater Enemy Appears

There can be nothing more serious than going into battle. Especially a battle where many might be killed. But at the same time it is hard to imagine anything more exciting. The Gungans may have been an odd and peculiar-looking people, but watching their soldiers rise dripping wet out of the swamp dressed in metal and leather body armor and riding powerful kaadu was really something.

Even more amazing were the Gungan soldiers atop the fambaas. I'd never seen creatures like these before. They were huge and looked like giant scaly salamanders. Each fambaa was outfitted with a shield generator that would (hopefully!) protect the Gungans from the battle droids' weapons.

While the Gungans marched bravely off toward the grassy hills beyond the swamp, Padmé, the Jedis, a small number of Naboo troops and fighter pilots, and I headed for the city. I knew Qui-Gon didn't want me to go, but with the whole planet about to go to war, there was no safe place to leave me.

We quietly entered the main city of Theed through secret passageways. For a moment I was struck by the beauty of the domed buildings and towers, but one look at the central plaza sent a shiver down my spine. Among the rubble of a recent battle, there were Trade Federation tanks and battle droids everywhere!

The sight of the enemy and the destruction it had already done made my throat grow tight. This wasn't a game. It wasn't a fight that could be settled with fists, or even a Podrace where someone wanted you dead. This was much, much bigger — an enemy of hundreds, maybe *thousands* of killing machines. And in the blink of an eye each one could vaporize a creature into a small heap of smoking ash.

My feet felt like they'd turned into lead. Suddenly my heart was pounding and I was having trouble breathing. What was I doing here? I'd gone along with Qui-Gon in the hope of learning to become a Jedi. I was nine years old! I didn't want to die.

As if he'd read my mind (maybe he had!) Qui-Gon turned and gave me an encouraging nod. I think he understood what I was feeling. But the look in his eyes said it was too late. There was no going back.

Our immediate destination was the central hangar complex, where the Naboo starfighters were kept. The hangar was connected to the Royal Palace. We had to get the Naboo pilots into those fighters and send them up to disable the Trade Federation Droid Control Ship. The lives of hundreds of Gungan soldiers depended on it.

As we divided into two groups, Qui-Gon took me aside and whispered that once we got inside the hangar, I should find a safe place to hide and stay there. I wanted to help him, but I had to follow his orders.

We waited while the other group of Naboo guards snuck across the central plaza. Padmé sent them a signal and the guards began to fire on the droids.

Instantly, the Trade Federation battle droids and tanks in the main plaza returned fire. Meanwhile Padmé's group rushed into the hangar. About a dozen bright yellow Naboo starfighters were inside. There were more droid guards in there and they started firing.

My ears were ringing with explosions and

sirens as a battle began for control of the Naboo fighters.

Following Qui-Gon's orders, I ran under a fighter and hid there. The air sizzled with blaster bolts and lasers being shot back and forth. I couldn't take my eyes off Padmé. She led her troops well and fought bravely, ducking laser blasts and taking out droids with her blaster.

A laser blast blew a hole in the floor just inches away from me. So close I felt its scorching heat. A shiver ran through me. If that blast had hit me, I'd be nothing more than a few chunks of charred flesh. Feeling light-headed, I backed deeper into my hiding place.

The fight continued with the Jedi Knights, Naboo guards, and pilots. They were pushing the Trade Federation droids back! Padmé gave the signal for the Naboo pilots and R2 units to get into the fighters. The next thing I knew, a Naboo pilot jumped into the fighter I was hiding under. He yelled at me to find a new place to hide, and before I knew it, the fighter was lifting off. I was in the middle of the hangar, totally unprotected!

With random laser blasts still rocketing over my head, I searched for a new place to hide.

I heard a whistle and turned to see the droid Artoo-Detoo in an unmanned fighter. He looked safe in the starfighter. In the middle of the battle, with no place else to go, it sounded like a good idea. I climbed in.

By now lots of Naboo starfighters were zooming out of the hangar. Out in the central plaza, a Trade Federation tank wheeled around and fired.

Ka-boom! I winced as a starfighter burst into flames and crashed. Luckily, the others managed to take off unharmed.

Having freed the starfighters, Padmé, the Jedi, and the Naboo guards turned toward the palace. The next part of the mission was to capture the viceroy. As they started out of the hangar, I began to climb out of the starfighter I'd been hiding in.

Suddenly Qui-Gon saw me and shouted that I was to stay inside the cockpit. I tried to argue with him, but he insisted that it was the safest place for me. I can't say I was happy about it, but I did as I was told.

I watched as the rest of the group headed for the doors leading out of the hangar. Suddenly they froze. In the doorway, blocking their path, stood the Sith Lord!

Thirteenth Entry
The Battle

His yellow eyes were intense, his red-and-black face terrifying. Padmé and the Naboo guards quickly backed away. Qui-Gon and Obi-Wan threw off their capes and ignited their lightsabers. For a split second I wondered how any warrior could fight off two Jedi. But then the dark warrior lit his saber. Both ends glowed ominously. His lightsaber was double-sided!

They started to fight. The fury of their battle was like nothing I'd ever seen. The Sith Lord could spring twenty meters in the air and do a flip while still fighting both Jedi. I was so amazed that I didn't even notice the other battle brewing behind us. Artoo whistled and I turned just in time to see three new Trade Federation droids roll into the hangar behind us. At first they looked like shiny metal wheels. But they quickly unfolded into heavily armed battle droids.

Padmé and the Naboo guards were trapped. The Sith Lord was fighting Obi-Wan and Qui-Gon at one end of the hangar and the destroyer droids were firing from the other end.

It looked bad. I knew I had to help and started hitting switches. Suddenly the starfighter lurched up and began to rise!

I steered the fighter toward the destroyer droids. I was going to get those three-legged death machines. All I had to do was find the trigger for the laser guns.

I stared down at the banks of brightly lit switches and buttons. Which one? Which *one?*

Oops! I pushed a button, but instead of firing lasers, the starfighter bucked. I must have tripped a stabilizer.

Meanwhile, the destroyer droids were moving in on Padmé and her team.

I tried another button.

Zap! Boom!

The nose lasers fired and a destroyer droid burst into smoke and flame.

All right! Artoo let out a whistle-cheer and I blasted another droid, and then another.

With the droids out of the way, Padmé and the

Naboo guards hurried into the palace. Meanwhile, the Sith Lord and the Jedi were locked in deadly combat.

Wham! My starfighter took a shot and heeled over. I jumped around. More droids had entered the hangar.

And now they were firing at me!

Suddenly we were in a storm of explosions. Artoo-Detoo was beeping at me like crazy. Of course I wanted the fighter's shield up! I just wasn't sure which . . .

Whoa! I hit a switch and we went from zero to sixty in a nanosecond. Artoo didn't have to tell me I'd accidentally flicked on the afterburners. I could feel it!

The good news was that I managed to steer the starfighter out of the hangar without crashing into any walls.

The bad news was that we were now rocketing upward and I still didn't know how to pilot a fighter!

We shot out of the city and over a vast grassy plain. Below us the Gungans and the Trade Federation battle droids were fighting fiercely. The plain was littered with shattered droids and wounded Gungans and kaadu. Lasers and energy balls were rocketing back and forth. The air was filled with explosions and smoke.

Artoo kept beeping at me, something about

the autopilot searching for other ships. But I couldn't see any.

Something was bothering him about those other ships. I told him if he didn't like where the autopilot was taking us, he should try to override the system.

Suddenly, out of the corner of my eye, I saw a bright explosion. There *were* ships out there! Naboo starfighters were battling Trade Federation fighters that had been sent out to protect the ship controlling the droid armies below.

In fact, the autopilot was steering us straight toward the enemy!

For a moment, I froze with disbelief. Equal parts of fear and excitement shot through me. What was I doing? A slave kid from Tatooine sitting at the controls of a lightspeed-fast starfighter hurtling toward an enemy battleship? If only Kitster could see this!

Out of nowhere a laser blast rocked my starfighter. I screamed at Artoo to get us off autopilot and he beeped back he just had. I grabbed the controls and swung the starfighter. It went left! Artoo had done it!

He beeped again, reminding me I had to go back. But I told him, no way. Qui-Gon had insisted I stay in this cockpit and that was exactly what I intended to do.

A Trade Federation fighter made the mistake of crossing into the airspace ahead of us. I got on his tail and had him in my sights. Blasting that guy out of the sky was going to be a cinch.

I just needed to know where the trigger for the fighter's laser cannon was!

Artoo beeped and I did what he told me to do.

The starfighter shot forward with a jolt. Instead of firing on the enemy fighter, I shot right past him. Now *he* was on *my* tail!

"Darn it, Artoo!" I yelled.

Artoo beeped a meek apology. The Trade Federation fighter now had us in his sights.

And that wasn't the worst of it. The really bad news was that we were headed straight for the Droid Control Ship!

I put the Naboo starfighter into a spin. And not a moment too soon. A laser blast from the fighter behind us shot over our left wing, barely missing us!

But we were still headed straight for the Control Ship. I yelled at Artoo that the only way out of this mess was the same way we'd gotten into it.

He beeped back and I hit a button, hoping this time it really was the starfighter's reverse thrusters.

It was! With a jolt, the starfighter slowed down. Now it was the Trade Federation fighter's turn to shoot past us.

Ka-boom! It crashed into the Control Ship.

I swung the starfighter around and stole a glance at the rest of the Naboo craft. They were taking shots at the Control Ship, but nothing was getting through the deflector shield.

This was bad. Unless they disabled that ship, the Gungan troops on the ground would be slaughtered. Artoo beeped again. Another Trade Federation fighter was on our tail!

Once again we were being chased back toward the Control Ship. I guess Artoo didn't approve of the way I was handling the starfighter because he kept beeping that this wasn't the same as Podracing.

As if I couldn't figure that out on my own!

Thwank! Something hit us from behind! It must have been a shot from the Trade Federation fighter. Artoo screeched as smoky sparks flew and lights flickered in the cockpit. Our starfighter went into an uncontrollable spin.

We were going to crash into the Control Ship!

By the time I got control of the starfighter, it was too late to avoid the giant ship. I had no choice but to steer toward the only open space ahead: a huge open hangar.

Suddenly we were inside the hangar, *inside* the Trade Federation Control Ship, still going much too fast. I was busy dodging transports, fighters, and other ships on the hangar deck.

Jamming my hand down on the reverse thrusters, I managed to stall the engines and bring the starfighter to a stop just before we hit the hangar wall.

For a second, everything was silent. Artoo gave me a low, worried whistle. Here we were dead center in the middle of enemy territory! I tried to restart the engines, but the whole instrument panel went red with warning lights.

I knew I must've blown something during the emergency landing. Or we'd just plain overheated.

But now we were surrounded by Trade Federation battle droids.

Not knowing what else to do, I ducked down in the cockpit. A battle droid captain came forward. He demanded to know who the pilot of our starfighter was. Artoo whistled back that he was the pilot. The battle droid appeared confused and asked to see identification.

Just then the lights on the cockpit control panel went from red to green!

I jumped up in the pilot's seat and flicked on the ignition. The starfighter powered up instantly.

The battle droid captain saw me in the cockpit and ordered that I come out or they'd shoot.

I answered by switching on the fighter's deflector shield. We started to rise and I swung the fighter around, knocking over the battle droid captain. The other droids were firing, but their shots were all deflected by the shield.

I aimed and fired at the droids. But I pressed the wrong button and set off two torpedoes!

The fighter recoiled as the torpedoes launched. With a jolt I realized it was too much and too close. My torpedoes missed the droids and shot down a hallway. I had a feeling once those torpedoes made contact, things were going to get very, very messy.

It was definitely time to say good-bye.

I swung the starfighter around and hit the thrusters. Unfortunately the hangar was full of droids by now and I had to knock a lot of them over. The funny thing was, it was *just like* Podracing!

KA-BOOM! As we reached the mouth of the hangar, a huge explosion erupted behind us.

Whoosh! The force of the blast pushed our starfighter right out of the hangar. I twisted around in my seat and watched as the Control Ship disappeared inside a huge ball of yellow and orange flame. Giant chunks of red-hot burning debris were shooting out into space in all directions.

We'd done it! We'd disabled the Trade Federation's Droid Control Ship!

Gripping the fighter's controls, I expected to

feel a surge of happiness as I steered the starfighter away. But I was suddenly overcome by a dark wave of pain and sadness.

At that moment I didn't know what had caused it. I only knew that something terrible was happening nearby.

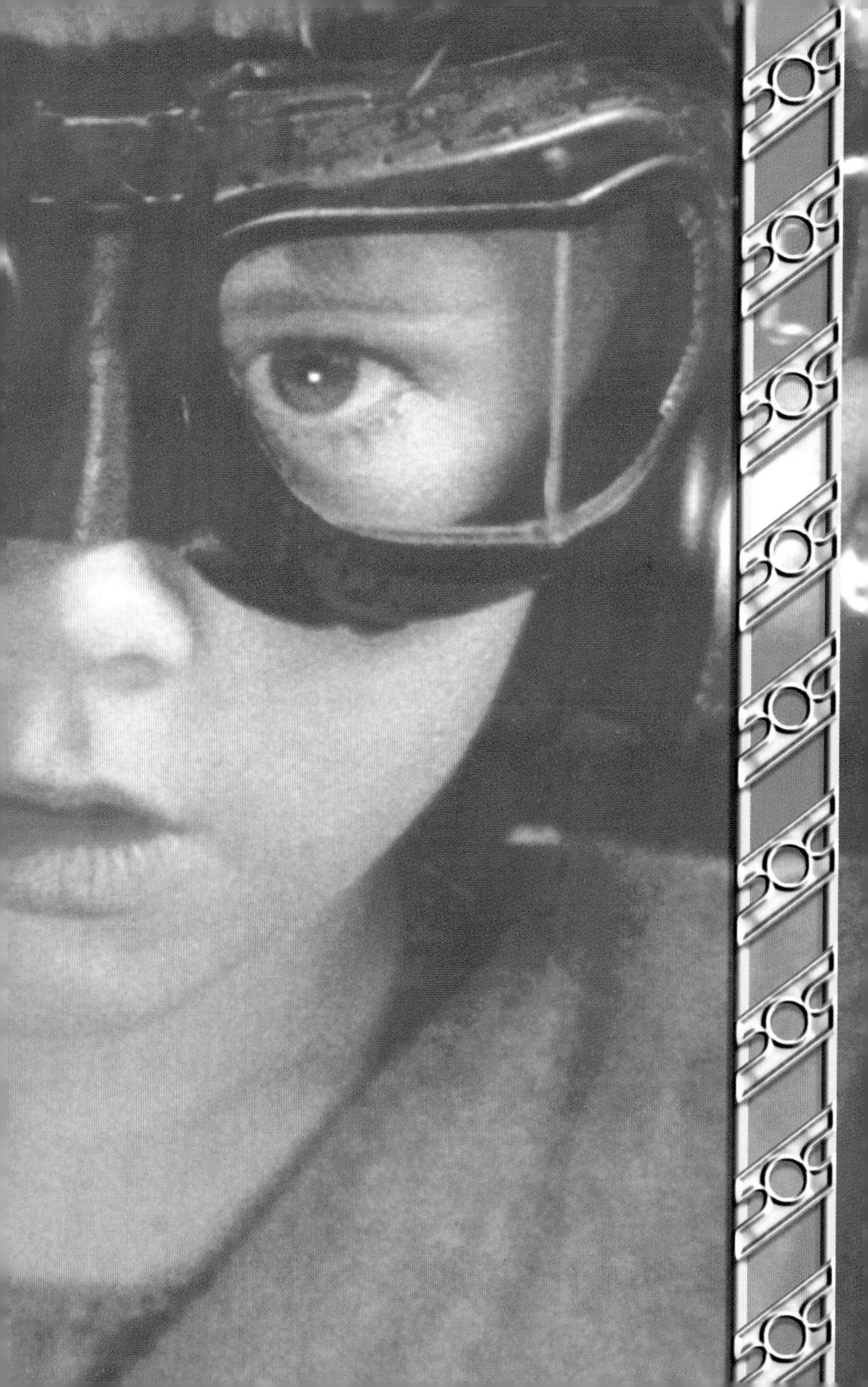

Fourteenth Entry
A Bitter Triumph

When the Control Ship blew up, the yellow Naboo startighters regrouped and headed back to Naboo. I wanted to speak to them via comlink, but my communications were dead. All I could do was limp back to Naboo behind them in my damaged fighter.

A little while later we skidded to a stop inside the palace hangar. A bunch of pilots and ground crew surrounded my fighter. When I opened the cockpit and stood up, their mouths dropped open. I could just about read their minds. How in the world had a kid my age managed to get into the Droid Control Ship and blow it up?

The funny thing was, I was asking myself the same question.

They helped me down from the starfighter and

told me the good news. When the ship exploded, all the Trade Federation battle droids on Naboo froze up, and the Queen was able to capture the viceroy. Together, the Gungans and the people of Naboo had won the battle. Their planet was free!

It should have been one of the happiest days of my life.

But just then a grim-faced guard entered the hangar. He'd heard that the Jedi Knights had defeated the Sith Lord. But in the battle, the older Jedi had been killed. . . .

I felt a terrible pang in my heart. Qui-Gon, my hero, my guardian, the one person who really understood . . . was gone. Suddenly I knew that the terrible, dark feeling I'd had in the starfighter was his death. I'd felt him go.

I closed my eyes and opened my mind, just as I had that night on Coruscant when Obi-Wan and Qui-Gon spoke. I could feel something. Qui-Gon was still there somehow. It was a shadow of what I'd felt before, but it was still there.

The funeral took place on the temple steps in the central plaza of Theed. It was sunset and the orange sun was dipping down toward the horizon. A large crowd was there: Queen Amidala and her handmaidens, the Jedi Council and other Jedi Knights who had known Qui-Gon Jinn personally, the troops of the Naboo, and the Gungan forces.

And, of course, Obi-Wan and me.

Qui-Gon's body was placed on a funeral pyre. We watched in silence as Qui-Gon Jinn disappeared in flames. Then white doves were released.

It was hard for me to watch. In the short time I'd known him, Qui-Gon had been more of a father to me than anyone I'd ever known. I thought back to the day I'd first met him on Tatooine. How we'd gone to my home to get out of the sandstorm. How I'd told him I suspected he was a Jedi Knight because of the lightsaber he carried. How he pretended maybe he'd simply killed a Jedi and taken the lightsaber. How I said no one could kill a Jedi Knight.

And how clearly I remembered that sad moment when he sighed and said, "I wish that were so."

As if even then he'd suspected . . .

I used the cuff of my uniform to wipe away tears. I felt Obi-Wan's hand on my shoulder.

"He is one with the Force, Anakin," he said softly. "You must let go."

I looked up into Obi-Wan's face and was surprised by what I saw. His expression was open and concerned. I could feel his caring as we shared the loss of someone we had both admired so much. With Qui-Gon's passing, something had changed between us.

I asked him what would happen to me now.

Nothing could have prepared me for Obi-Wan's answer.

"I am your Master now," he said, tightening his grip on my shoulder. "You will become a Jedi. I promise."

Time to Go

Obi-Wan just stuck his head in the doorway and said that we are leaving in five minutes. It's time for this journal to end.

So much has happened. I will never be the same as I was on Tatooine. It is clear that my life will be different from Kitster's, different from my mother's, different from anyone's that I've known before. I have faith in Obi-Wan's promise: My training will begin soon.

My travels will continue. I will go to planets and have experiences I cannot begin to imagine. I am both frightened and excited.

Wherever the path leads, I am ready.